The Prelude of Ella and Micha

JESSICA SORENSEN

For information:

jessicasorensen.com

Cover Design and Photography: Mae I Design

www.maeidesign.com

The Prelude of Ella and Micha (The Secret #0.5)

ISBN: 978-1499576900

Prologue

Ella

I remember when I was younger and everything seemed so simple. Not that my life was ever simple, but there was a time when I didn't have to worry about the future or how my life would end up. Only the day ahead of me mattered. As long as I knew the sun would rise in the morning and set in the evening, everything would turn out okay. There was a sense of freedom in that, in the lack of concern in what lay ahead.

"If you beat me through the sprinkler," my best friend Micha shouts from across the front lawn of his house, "I'll let you have the last piece of cake."

"But my mom said not to get wet!" I holler back, inching across the grass. "I don't want to get grounded again!"

"Where's your daredevil side?" Micha yells back, leaning over as if he's on a track, getting ready to race.

Water rains across the grass between us, daring me to

do it, daring me to get wet even though I know I'll get in trouble.

"Fine!" Without warning, I sprint across the grass, water soaking my bare feet, shorts, shirt, and hair.

Micha laughs as he runs into the spray with me. "You cheated!" he calls out, chasing after me as I dance around in a circle, staying just outside the sprinklers' reach. "That's not fair."

"No way!" I laugh. "It was totally fair and now you owe me a piece of cake."

We laugh as we keep running around, chasing something that can only be seen by our childlike minds. There's an invisible sense of freedom, with no regard to the consequences of what will happen after I have to go inside and show my mother that I disobeyed.

That freedom was something that stuck with me for at least a year or two.

But then I got older.

Wiser.

The complications of life that I was blinded to at such a young age became painfully visible. It didn't happen slowly, but as quickly as the beat of a heart, like a blindfold had been ripped off my eyes. Suddenly, I could see that bad choices sometimes equaled irrevocable outcomes, and I spent a long time blaming myself for what happened.

Looking back, I realize the painful events I went through weren't in my control. Sometimes things just happen, and we can't change them. Nor was it always my fault. But at seventeen years old, my mind wasn't ready to grasp the concept. If it had, maybe things would have been a bit easier. Perhaps I wouldn't have fled and left everything—everyone—behind.

In the end, I did run, and it irrevocably altered the entire course of my future.

Chapter 1

14 years old...

Ella

I trudge home from school an hour early with a dark, bluish-purple bruise splattered across my cheek, a thin cut across my bottom lip, and a pink detention slip inside my backpack. It's not the first time I've been sent home over a fight, and I'm sure it won't be my last. I have a knack for fights. Not because I'm a bully. In fact, I'm the polar opposite and tend to get into fights with the bullies whenever they're picking on someone. I'm not trying to be a hero or anything. I just have a vast dislike for people getting picked on. Plus, I like the rush that comes from jumping in and doing something instead of standing by and watching.

There are always consequences for my actions, although not usually from my parents. By the time I get home, my mother will probably be sedated from the intense meds she's on for her Bipolar Disorder. And my dad will either be at work or at the bar trying to drink away the fact that my mother has a mental illness. Neither of them will care about the condition of my face or the detention slip.

No, my ass is going to get reamed by Micha Scott, aka my best friend since forever. Aka my best friend who thinks I'm his responsibility for whatever reason.

I still have a couple of hours before school releases and he shows up at my house so when I arrive home, I decide to de-stress after chores. The first thing on my to-do list, though, is a painkiller to alleviate my headache.

Going into the kitchen, I drop my backpack on the table, grab a bottle from the medicine cabinet, and pop two pills into my mouth. Then I fetch some ice from the freezer and place it on my eye, holding it there while I hurry and pick up the week's worth of garbage littering the floor. Most of the contents that end up in the trash bag are empty bottles of vodka, tequila, and beer. I do find some stale takeout wedged between the fridge and the counter along with a few pots and pans on the table that are caked with month old grease. The fridge was open when I entered the kitchen, probably left that way by my mother. Thankfully, there's hardly any food inside that could have spoiled.

After I shut the fridge, I sort through the past due bills I collected from the mailbox and try to figure out which ones to pay this week. Then I make out the checks, leaving the signature line blank for my dad to sign whenever he gets home. It's exhausting thinking about money, and the process makes me kind of regret getting sent home early.

So much for de-stressing.

Once the kitchen is polished and the checks are filled out, I lose the ice pack and peek in on my mom in her bedroom. She's sprawled out on the mattress, snoring, with her arm draped over the edge of the bed and a bottle of pills next to her. Tiptoeing to the bed, I pick up the bottle and count how many pills there are inside. Three less than from this morning, which means she's okay and hasn't taken too many.

Keeping track of the pills is something I've had to do for a couple of months now, ever since she accidentally took too many and ended up in the emergency room. After they pumped her stomach, the doctors and nurses put her on suicide watch for twenty-four hours, even though my mother insisted the overdose was accidental—that she'd forgotten she'd already taken her dose in the morning. The doctors didn't seem to believe her, but I do because there's no way she'd intentionally want to die. How could she? She's my mother.

I put the medicine bottle in the bathroom cabinet then leave the bedroom and wander into my room. The purple walls are freshly painted with black skulls thanks to Micha, who decided the other day that my room was too girly for him. It's cool, though. I dig the skulls. Plus, I'm not a girlie girl at all. My typical outfit is holey jeans and a dark T-shirt. Sometimes I wear a hoodie. I never wear makeup and almost always put my auburn hair up in a ponytail because doing anything else with it is a pain in the ass. Sneakers are my choice of footwear. Right now, the pair of shoes I'm wearing match my walls.

Collecting my sketch book and pencil from the dresser, I flop down on my bed and attempt to unwind by getting lost in my art. But, after a while, the silence of the house gets to me, so I turn on my stereo that's about twenty years old. I cruise the radio stations and choose a classic one because my only other options are country and heavy metal.

Then I situate myself on my bed again and continue working on the sketch that's for my art class. A vase. So boring.

Finally, I decide to take a break and flip the page to one of my own projects, one of Micha that I will never, *ever* show him, because it's embarrassing. I have no idea how he'd react if he knew I was drawing him, and I never want to find out. But I can't seem to stop—he's always stuck in my head.

Ten minutes later, my hand moves mindlessly across the crisp page, creating sharp angles, soft curves, dark shading. The portrait creation goes on for what seems like forever, and when I finally blink back to reality, I feel more content than I have all day.

Deciding to stop for now, I shake the cramp out of my hand and get up and stretch before cranking up the music. "We Got the Beat" by The Go-Go's blares through the speakers. I stand up on the bed and rock out, jumping up and down on the mattress and spinning in circles. Mid chorus, I tug the elastic from my hair and start head banging, really getting into the beat. If I was musically talented, I would so be a drummer or a singer, but art is my forte. Music is Micha's talent. He can play the guitar like a pro, and his voice is the most beautiful sound I've ever heard in all my fourteen years. Of course, I don't tell him this. He'd tease me and call me a silly girl if I divulged the sappy side of me.

As I'm in the middle of a very awesome air guitar solo, I notice a gentle breeze has fluttered into the room.

"Dammit," I curse, knowing what the chill means. What I don't know is whether it's better if I just continue dancing until maybe Micha leaves or stop and face the embarrassment. Then again, I really don't want him to leave, never do.

Pressing my lips together, I stop shaking and shimmying, plaster on my best smile, and turn on the bed to face him, trying to appear all sweet and innocent, like he didn't just catch me rocking out to 80s rock.

His tall, gangly figure lingers near the window, the place he always enters my room by climbing up the tree just outside. He's sporting black jeans and a matching T-shirt decorated with a red skull and crossbones, and his sandy blond hair is a little on the longish side, hanging across his forehead and in his eyes. Micha's eyes are actually super intense, a fierce aqua blue color, similar to the ocean.

"Hey." I casually wave, plopping down onto the mattress with a bounce. Then I lean over to turn the radio down.

His gaze instantly darts to the fresh shiner on my cheek "Did you have fun today?" he asks, folding his arms and reclining against the wall as his stare bores into me.

I shrug, scratching my injured cheek. "You know how I love to dance."

He shakes his head, but his lips quirk, a smile threatening to slip through. "I'm not talking about the dancing." He stands up straight and crosses the room toward my bed. "I'm talking about you getting into a fight today with Diana Rollinson."

"Oh, that." I stand up and square my shoulders, hating that I have to tip my head back to look at him. It's not like I'm short or anything. Up until about three months ago, I was taller than him. But, almost overnight, he shot up and now has me by about six inches. "Look, I know you hate it

14

when I get into fights, but Diana was being a bitch to Sandy, who barely says two words to anyone."

"So you were defending someone's honor. By getting punched in the face."

"Hey." I cross my arms and glare at him. "I got in quite a few swings before this thing happened." I point at the bruise on my cheek, "Which, FYI, came from when she pushed me into the lockers, not from her fists. She can't even punch, total hair puller."

He's struggling not to laugh while remaining my fourteen-year-old voice of reason, more mature for his age than most guys. "What about the cut on your lip?"

I elevate my hands in front of me and make scratching motions in the air. "She's a total clawer, too." I sigh when he continues to stare at me without so much as a tiny grin. "Look, I'm sorry, okay? But it's not that big of a deal. I only got sent home early today."

His head slants to the side as he gently brushes his finger across the tender area on my cheek. "You're going to ruin that pretty face of yours if you keep this up."

I stick out my tongue as my cheeks heat. I loathe compliments, even when they're meant sarcastically. "Ha, ha, you're a freaking riot, Micha Scott."

He presses his hand to his chest, giving me an innocent look. "I call you pretty, and you stick your tongue out at me? Seriously, Ella May, you just broke my heart."

And, just like that, the tension breaks after only a minute of chatting.

Always does.

Which is why I need Micha in my life.

Even if he tries to be my voice of reason.

"I'm sure I did," I retort sarcastically with an eye roll, which he seems to find more amusing than anything. "Okay, I'm sorry I got into a fight and got my *pretty*"—I roll my eyes again— "face ruined. But I won't promise that I'm not going to do it again, because I don't make promises I know I won't keep."

"One of these days, you're going to get into trouble." His gaze drifts over my shoulder to my bed. "You know that." His forehead creases as he studies something behind me.

I twist around to see what he's looking at and realize I

left my sketchbook out on my bed, opened to the page displaying the detailed sketch of Micha sitting under a massive oak tree. His head is tipped down, he has a pen in his hand, and there's a notebook on his lap that he's scribbling lyrics into.

"Oh, shit." I leap for the bed and snatch it up, pressing the drawing to my chest.

"What was that?" he asks as I roll over on my back, hugging the book to my chest as I look up at him.

"Nothing," I say quickly, which is clearly a mistake.

He kneels down on the bed, putting a knee on each side of me, like he does whenever we wrestle. "Come on, Ella May, let me see," he says in the sweet voice he only uses whenever he's trying to get his way.

"That voice doesn't work on me." I attempt to slide upwards on the bed and out from under him. "It only works on girls like Diana."

He chuckles, but doesn't budge, and I continue to wiggle, fighting to get out from underneath him.

"Come on. Let me go," I plead.

"Not until you let me see whatever it is you're hiding

17

from me."

"No way." My grasp tightens on the book. "My drawings are private. You know that." Which is kind of a lie. Only drawings of him are private.

He considers what I've said then, with a sigh, he climbs off me. "Oh, fine. You win."

"I always win," I say, shooting him a cocky grin.

"Well, if you're going to act that way." He dives back on me and starts tickling me until I drop the sketchbook.

"You are the meanest boy ever!" I laugh so hard tears stream down my cheeks.

He grins as he releases me and backs up off the bed. The smile slips from his face as he catches sight of my sketchbook and the drawing I was trying to hide from him. His expression is unreadable—confused and kind of ... flattered?

"You're drawing me?" He looks at me with curiosity written all over his face.

My cheeks erupt with heat as I flop back on the bed and stare up at the Chevelle poster on my ceiling. "I was bored, okay? The art class projects are too cliché, and I needed to work on improving my life drawings." *Liar, liar*.

I wait for him to call me out because he knows me well enough that he can.

He leans over and picks the sketchbook up off the floor. "You want to go to the park with me and hang out for a bit?" he asks as he tosses the book onto my dresser.

I prop up on my elbows and arch my eyebrows at him. "What? No snarky remarks about how my drawing means I'm secretly in love with you? Or that I think you're so dreamy?" I make a joking swoony face then gag.

He snorts a laugh then waves me off. "Nah, I don't need to repeat something we both already know." When I pinch his arm, he laughs. "Come on. Come to the park with me." He pouts out his lip. "Pretty please. It'll be fun."

I roll my eyes but easily give in, knowing he'll keep looking at me like that until I do. Besides, I'm never one to pass up the opportunity to get out of the house.

"Fine," I surrender, sitting up. "But only because I have nothing better to do."

Grinning like a goof, he offers me his hand and hauls me to my feet. He doesn't let go, slipping his fingers through mine as he leads me out of my room and down the stairs.

The holding hands gesture is nothing new. Ever since we became best friends ten years ago, he usually either has his arm around me, is holding my hand, tickling me, or touching my hair. Sometimes, I think he doesn't even realize he's doing it. Renee, this girl that I sometimes hang out with, thinks it's because Micha has a crush on me and is secretly in love with me. I laugh whenever she tells me this because Micha isn't in love with me, at least, not like the way she means it. He's already kissed like three girls, and I don't see him ever trying to kiss me. Well, except for maybe on the cheek.

"So how bad did Diana look after the fight?" Micha asks after we've exited my house and entered the neighborhood we've both grown up in. "I'm guessing you got her pretty good."

"Of course I did," I reply as we start up the sidewalk lined with rundown homes. It's late afternoon and most of the area appears like it's sleeping. But that's typical for Star Grove. Around ten is when the yards and houses will be flooding with loud noises of parties taking place. "Both her eyes were swollen."

He smiles then leans over and gives me a quick kiss on the head. Then we continue our journey down the sidewalk in comfortable silence. When we arrive at the desolate playground, we hike across the dry grass to the rusty swing set in the middle. We each sit down in our own seat and then run back and pump our legs, swinging high toward the tip of the nearby trees.

"Do you ever wonder what life would be like on the other side of the mountains?" I ask as I stare at the rolling hills that encompass the town.

"Of course I do." He kicks his legs, ascending higher as he tips his head back toward the grey sky.

"Do you think we'll ever get to find out?" I grasp the chains as I soar. "Do you ever think we'll get out of here?"

"Of course we will," he says. "There's no way we can stay here in this stupid town forever."

"Yeah, but I'm not sure if I'll ever be able to leave my mother behind," I mutter. "I mean, who will take care of her if I'm not around? My dad's not capable of doing so, and Dean's not ever going to." Dean is my older brother who is probably home about twice a week, only coming back to change his clothes. I have no idea where he stays during the rest of the week.

"So what? They can figure that out." Micha's jaw is set tight, and his blue eyes burn fiercely. "You're not staying here. You're leaving with me."

"We'll see," I sigh. "At eighteen, we might not even be friends anymore. I've heard high school is rough."

He's silent for a while, contemplating what I've said. It's not like I really believe high school will ruin our friendship. I just don't believe I'll ever be able to leave Star Grove. It's just hope, and I've hoped for a lot of things I've never gotten.

Micha abruptly plants his feet into the dirt below us and skids to a halt. Without uttering a word, he reaches over and grabs the chain of my swing, causing me to jerk to a stop, spin around, and crash straight into him.

"Holy crap," I say breathlessly as I clutch onto the chains. "What the heck did you do that for?"

"Because I want you to understand something," he

says intensely. "You and I are going to leave this town. *To-gether*." He pauses when I stare at him with doubt. Then he thoughtfully adds, "In fact, we're going to make a pact on it. Right here. Right now."

"Haven't we made a ton of those already?"

"So what's one more?"

"Good point." Still, I'm a pessimist when it comes to ever escaping this town. Most people born and raised here never leave. But I'll try anything to boost the odds from not being a statistic. Plus, the future he's proposed doesn't sound all that bad. In fact, it sounds nice. "All right, let's make a pact."

He grins then spits into his palm before extending his hand toward me. "Ready?"

"You know, we really need to come up with a less disgusting way to make these pacts." But I still spit into my palm and place my hand in his.

"So who's going to say it this time?" he asks. "You or me?"

"I'll do the honors." I consider my word choice. "Okay, so here's the deal. As soon as we turn eighteen, we rummage all our money together and get the hell out of here. No questions asked."

"And where will we live?" he asks amusedly.

I shrug. "How about by the ocean? We've never seen it before. It might be cool."

"The ocean sounds nice." He muses over something. "Sounds good to me. Leave, go to the ocean. You can become a famous artist, and I'll become a musician."

"And we'll make sure we have better lives," I add. "Ones we're happy with."

"Agreed," he says and then we shake on it. "Although, I have to say that I'm not sad about everything in my life right now."

Unlike me, Micha has a stable parent—his mother who I sometimes like to pretend is my own mother when I'm having a rough day. Still, things haven't always been easy for him. His father walked out on Micha and his mom about eight years ago, and it was both financially and emotionally hard on them.

"I'm talking about you," Micha adds, letting go of my hand.

I blink my attention back to him. "What?"

He winks at me before walking back with his fingers wrapped around the chains. "You, Ella May, are the creation of my happiness." He lifts his legs and shoots forward.

I roll my eyes as I back up. "You are so stinking cheesy sometimes. No other fourteen-year-old boy talks the way you do."

"How do you know that?" he questions as he swings back and forth. "Are their more fourteen-year-old guys in your life that I don't know about?"

I shrug as I launch forward. "Ethan. And he doesn't talk like that."

"He might."

"Yeah, right."

"Hey, he's my best friend," he teases as we level out and swing harmoniously together. "For all you know, he could talk like that when you're not around."

I jut out my lip, pouting. "Hey, I thought I was your best friend."

"No way," he says in all seriousness. "You're way more than that."

I flop my head back, gagging. "God, stop with the cheesy pickup lines. It's making me nauseous."

"Fine, but only if you play truth with me."

"Fine, but only if I get to ask the first question."

He smiles. "Be my guest."

I contemplate. "So, Micha Scott, just how many girls have you kissed now?"

He suspiciously glances at me from the corner of his eye. "You already know the answer to that since you asked me the same question the last time we played this."

"Yeah, but it's been a few weeks since then." I lift my shoulder and give a half shrug. "And I heard a rumor yesterday."

"About what?"

"That you and Kessa kissed behind the school during third period."

He shoots me a dirty look. "Fuck no. I would never kiss Kessa Finlany. Who told you that?"

"Kessa."

He frowns, staring ahead at the playground. "Well, that never happened. And it will never happen."

"Noted." I swing higher, and he matches my move, stretching his legs toward the sky. "So the number is still three?"

"Yep, still three." He grows silent, his face contorting in deep thought as he debates his question for me. When he arrives at his conclusion, a slow grin expands across his face, and I know I'm in big trouble. "So, Ella May, just how many boys have *you* kissed?"

The chilly breeze stings at my warm cheeks. "That's not a fair question."

"And why's that?"

"Because you already know the answer to that."

"And how do you figure that? I mean, for all I know, something could have changed since the last time I asked you."

"You know it hasn't," I say, feeling stupid. "I pretty much don't hang out with anyone but you."

His brow cocks and amusement dances in his eyes. "So the number's still zero?"

I grip the chains, annoyed. "See, you already knew the answer, so that wasn't a fair question."

"Why? It's my wasted turn." He sticks his feet to the ground again and this time grinds to a slow halt. Then he just sits there motionlessly as he watches me swing back and forth.

"What are you doing?" I wonder as I kick my feet higher. Strands of my auburn hair slip lose from my ponytail and surround my face. "Why are you looking at me like that?"

He muses over something, rubbing his jawline. "I have a proposition for you."

"No way," I instantly respond. "I know better than to agree to your propositions."

"Just hear me out first," he says, using the voice again. "Then you can make your decision."

Sighing, I plant my feet in the dirt to stop beside him, knowing he won't give up until I at least agree to hear whatever it is he's thinking. "Fine, what's your proposition?"

"I propose," he starts, seeming the slightest bit uneasy, which is weird for him, "that I be your first kiss."

I snort a big, old, pig laugh. "Ha, very funny. For a

moment, I thought you were going to be serious."

"I am being serious." His expression matches his words.

And my expression plummets. "W-what? Why would you ever ask me that? Or want to do that?"

He shrugs. "You have to get your first kiss over sometime, so why not do it with me?"

I scrunch up my nose. "Because you're … you." I don't mean for it to come out so rude. Luckily, Micha knows me well enough not to take it personally.

His lips quirk. "And what's wrong with me? Am I too hideous for you?"

"No," I sputter quickly, and he laughs. "That's not it at all. I'm just …"

"You're just what, waiting around for the perfect guy to show up? Like Grantford Davis?"

"Ew." I swat his arm, and his laughter increases. "No way. I would never, *ever* use my first kiss on him. He's so weird and gross."

"A lot of the guys our age are weird and gross. Except me."

"That's not entirely true," I say then pause. "But I guess, out of all the guys at our school, you are the least gross."

"Okay, then," he states like this solves the problem. "Let's do this."

Do what?

Kiss Micha?

God, I've barely even hugged anyone, let alone kissed anyone.

I should protest more—I know I should—but a part of me is curious as to why the hell kissing is such a big deal.

"You promise you won't make fun of me or anything?"

He gives me a *really* look. "Do I ever make fun of you?"

I throw back the look he just gave me. "All the time."

"But that's just for fun." He waves me off. "I don't mean any of it."

"Just promise me you won't tease me, and I'll do it. In fact, you have to promise not to ever bring it up." I spit into my hand. "Make a pact on it."

30

He considers my proposal for about a half a second then spits into his palm and shakes on it. "Deal."

As we pull our hands away, I grow nervous because now I have to actually kiss him. And not just kiss *him*, but kiss my first guy *ever*.

"Are you sure you want to do this?" I double check, wiping my palm on my jeans. "Because I don't know what I'm doing."

"I'll show you." He's already leaning in, his intense aqua eyes zeroed in on my lips.

My heart dances like a crazy person in my chest, and I feel like I'm going to throw up. "Micha, I ..." I trail off, sucking in a huge breath as his lips touch mine. My fingers tense around the chains and my whole body stiffens while I try to figure out what on earth I'm supposed to be doing. Clearly not just sitting here, frozen.

"Relax," Micha whispers, putting a small bit of space between our lips.

Thinking the kiss is over, I let out a quiet, relieved breath. But the relief is short lived because, a microsecond later, his head dips forward and his lips brush against mine again. Only, this time, it's different. This time, he slips his tongue into my mouth.

Oh, my God, his tongue is in my mouth.

Micha Scott's *tongue is in my mouth.*

And I just touched my tongue to his.

Before I can even register what's happening, we're kissing. And I mean full on French-kissing. It goes on for what feels like minutes, our knees knocking against each other as Micha plays with my hair and continues to kiss me. Unfamiliar feelings prickle inside me, ones I'm pretty sure I've never felt before, and that terrifies the living daylights out of me. They make me feel so...

Out of control.

And Micha is supposed to be my stability.

I'm about to pull away because I can't take the terror hounding inside me anymore when a loud crash echoes from nearby and we both jerk apart, wide-eyed and gasping for air. My cheeks start to burn and even Micha appears embarrassed, which has never happened before—at least, from what I've seen.

Seconds later, reality crashes over me.

Oh, my God, I just kissed my best friend.

The silence that follows is painful, and I worry that everything is going to change. Be ruined. He won't want to be my friend anymore, and if I don't have him, I have no one.

I wish I never kissed him.

"Well, that was interesting," Micha remarks, touching his fingers to his lips as he chuckles.

"Interesting, as in bad?" I ask, nervous for unclear reasons.

He swiftly shakes his head. "No way. Not bad at all." That's all he says before he runs back and starts swinging again. "So, did you hear that Ethan and Jane are going out?"

Confused by the abrupt subject change, I slowly let the swing crawl forward. "No."

"Yeah, he told me the other day." He starts chatting about who's going out with who, updating me on the latest middle school gossip, but I zone out, my thoughts floating back to the kiss.

It felt so right yet so wrong. So good yet so terrifying.

33

Are things going to change after this? Do I look as awkward as I feel on the inside? What is happening to me? Micha usually calms me down, but right now, being close to him is freaking me out. Although, in a good way, a way I don't know how to handle.

As my thoughts and emotions start to jumble together, I feel like a huge mess. Finally, I arrive at a conclusion: never again. Never will I kiss Micha again.

Never, ever will I risk our friendship and our beautiful future together again.

Chapter 2

16 years old...

Micha

There's a certain moment in my life that changed my future forever. It blindsided me, but if I really had been looking to begin with, I would have seen it coming. It started with a simple surfacing of emotion.

My emotions for Ella have gotten way stronger. The thought comes out of nowhere while I sit in the waiting room, waiting for Ella to come out from the emergency area. She fell off the roof only hours earlier and blacked out. For a second, I thought she was dead thanks to my drunk friend Ethan yelling that she was. I seriously about had a fucking heart attack, and in that moment, something changed between us. I thought she was dead and realized I can't live without her.

I can never lose her. God, it hurts to even think about it.

When she finally walks out into the waiting room with a cast on her arm, another thought strikes me out of nowhere.

My emotions for Ella have gotten so strong I can hardly think straight when I'm near her.

"Are you okay?" I ask, quickly standing as she reaches me. My heart is slamming inside my chest while I scan her entire body for any more injuries.

She tiredly nods. "Yeah, I just broke my arm"—she elevates her arm that's covered in a cast—"nothing too serious."

I stare at her, probably for too long. Then I wrap my arms around and pull her in for a too tight hug. "Don't ever do that shit again." My voice is hoarse, but I'm too exhausted and worried to give a shit.

She tensely puts her good arm around me and pats me on the back. "Micha, it's not that big of a deal. I've snowboarded off a roof before." She starts to draw back, but my arms constrict around her.

"I don't care," I whisper in her hair. "Promise me you'll be more careful from now on. And stay off roofs."

She sighs, relaxing into me. "Yes, voice of reason."

I pull back enough to look down at her. "Voice of reason?"

She shrugs. "That's what I call you sometimes when you're trying to take care of me."

"I'm always trying to take care of you." I turn for the door and slip an arm around her back, refusing to let her go. *Ever.* "Now, come on. Let's get you home and take care of you some more."

***

I was hoping by the next morning my feelings would go back to normal, that Ella and I would go back to normal. But, if anything, it's gotten worse.

Nothing is ever going to be normal again. At least, not with me.

The revelation comes to me abruptly while I'm writing lyrics in my bedroom. At sixteen years old, the words pouring out of me are soul bearing, defining, and fucking startling, like a lightning bolt to the heart. And, the thing is, it's not the first time I've written about Ella like this. My very first song was about her, too. At the time, it didn't mean anything, but now I have to question what the cause is behind my emotional words dedicated to her.

The entire time I pen, all I'm thinking about is how I felt when I thought Ella had died. My hand actually begins to tremble, and my nerves only amplify when I reread my poetry. Where did these lyrics stem from? How the hell did I go from scribbling about desolation to writing about the person who means the world to me?

I'm so fucking scared.

And kind of excited.

"Are you okay?" Ella asks with concern from across the room.

It's not like anything has visibly changed between us since last night. She still slept in the bed with me, fully dressed with a bit of space between our bodies, even though every one of my limbs craved to eliminate any amount of air between us. We woke up and had breakfast, chatted with my mother, then went back to my room to draw and write lyrics.

Her sketchbook is open on her lap while I strum my guitar and pencil down the rest of the mind-blowing lyrics.

But the words only carry half my attention. The other half is on her, watching her uninjured hand move wildly across the paper, even as she stares at me with those big, beautiful green eyes of hers.

When did I realize her eyes are so beautiful? And how lean and long her legs are? How smooth her skin looks? How much I want to touch her smooth skin ... kiss her lips ... bite her flesh ... watch her hand trace across my body ...

Suddenly, that hand of hers stops, and she sets the pencil down. "Micha, what's up?" She sits up in the beanbag chair. "You look like you've seen a ghost."

I blink my attention from my dirty fantasies, my fingers halting on the guitar strings. "What?" Her concern is severely distracting to the point that I can barely focus. That's the thing with Ella: she always cares about me enough to check on me, and when she's staring at me with concern, like she is now, it's difficult to even breathe.

Her forehead creases as she leans toward the bed, scrutinizing me. "Are you high?"

High on you.

Where do I come up with this shit?

I adjust the guitar in my lap. "No, why?"

She shrugs then relaxes back, tucking a strand of her auburn hair behind her ear. The movement causes my heartbeat to quicken and blood to roar in my eardrums.

"You just seem distracted," she responds. "And you look kind of pale."

"Being high doesn't make me pale." I cringe at the thickness in my voice. I'm never awkward around girls, and now I'm about as nervous as a debater with severe stage fright. "And I'm always a little distracted when I'm working on a song, especially when I'm about to finish one." *About my feelings for you.*

"That's awesome." She smiles brightly. It's the most beautiful sight I've ever seen. "Can I see what you have down so far?" She sets her sketchbook aside on the floor and kneels in front of me.

When she reaches for my notepad, I jerk back, tucking it behind me while dropping the guitar onto the bed.

"What the heck, Micha? Are you …?" She peers up at me with glossy eyes, like she's about to cry. "Are you mad at me about something?"

"What!" I exclaim. "No, it's just ..." I think about the lyrics that just flowed out of me, as though my subconscious was speaking to me, whispering things I never realized until now. "I'm not mad, I just ... don't want you to read these until they're finished." It's only when she starts to relax that I do, as well.

"Well, if you need to talk to me," she says, sitting back on her heels, "I'm here for you. I know today's a rough day."

My brows knit as I set the notepad down on the mattress and scoot to the edge of the bed, planting my feet on the floor. "Why? What's today?"

"Um, ten years since your dad left." She folds her arms on top of my knees and looks up at me. The contact is almost unbearable, though in the best way possible.

Breathe, you dumb ass. It's just a girl touching you, nothing more, nothing less.

Except the girl touching you remembered your father took off ten years ago today. The girl knows and cares about your past.

"I'm fine." I wave her off then get to my feet. "But we

should go do something fun."

"Okay," she easily agrees. Ella is usually up for fun, no matter the circumstances. She bounds to her feet and closes her sketchbook before reaching for her leather jacket. "What are you up for tonight? Racing? Dinner at the diner? We can go to that party downtown that people were talking about."

I reach for my hoodie on my bedpost. "A party sounds kind of nice." I glance down at her cast. "As long as you feel up to it." *Maybe the noise will drown out my freaking alarming thoughts and feelings.*

"My arm feels fine." She reaches for the doorknob but dithers. "But, if we go to the party, will you promise not to act like a weirdo like you did at the last one? Because it wigs me out."

I slip on my jacket. "I never act like a weirdo at parties, do I?"

She stares me down from over her shoulder. "The last party we went to, you almost beat Jonny Moylton's ass because he was"—she lets go of the doorknob to make air quotes—"dry humping me. Seriously, Micha. You're starting to act like a jealous boyfriend."

My frown deepens as I painfully realize how right she is. I was extremely pissed off watching Jonny touch her like that, and I acted crazy. I'll do it again, too.

"Well, he was asking for it," I tell her, unable to stop myself. "He shouldn't have been touching you like that."

"That's not really for you to decide." She turns for the door again. "Guys are allowed to touch me, Micha. In case you haven't noticed, I am a girl."

Oh, I've noticed. Boy, have I fucking noticed.

"It is too for me to decide who gets to touch you," I mutter then cringe when I realize I said it aloud.

She fires a death glare at me. "What is your problem? I don't get it. You've been acting really ... weird and pouty the last few weeks."

I want to tell her I'll stop. I'll control myself. Control my emotions. But I'd be lying to her, and I never want to be that guy to her, the one who feeds her bullshit like every other dude in her life.

"You know what I'm craving?" I say, nervously scratching my neck. "Some of that cheesecake my mom made you for your birthday."

She blinks once at the abrupt subject change, but then her eyes fill with hunger at the mention of cheesecake, just like I knew they would—Ella loves her cheesecake. "Is there any left?"

I nod as I zip up my jacket. "Yeah. Let's sneak a few slices before we head out."

She smiles, which is a rarity, before pulling on the door. When she gets it halfway open, though, she unexpectedly pauses, and I almost end up running into her.

"Maybe we should stop by the diner to get something to eat before the party," she suggests, turning her head ever so slightly.

We're so close our lips almost touch, and it takes every single bit of strength I have not to lower my lips and devour her. My hands curl into fists, and I breathe through my nose, trying to keep my erratic airflow as discreet as possible.

"I mean, if we're going to be drinking, which I'm guessing we are, we can't do it on empty, cheese-cake only stomachs; otherwise, we'll relive last month's puking party we had when we get home."

"Good idea. I am kind of hungry." I can barely form words because her vanilla scent is overpowering all of my senses, drowning me with an emotion that terrifies me.

She slowly nods, carefully eyeing me over. "Are you positive you're okay? You seem kind of ... weirdo-ish again."

A slow exhale eases from my lips as I gather up what little sanity I have left, then I plaster on a smile. "Yeah, I'm great. Better than great. I'm fucking spectacular."

What I really want to say is *"No, I'm not fine, fucking great, or spectacular. Nor will I ever be again. Because I think I'm falling in love with my best friend, who quite possibly will never love me back."*

***

Three hours later, my thoughts about loving Ella stream through my mind louder than the music blasting throughout the packed house. Louder than the sea of alcohol swimming inside me. Louder than my heart beat, which is practically screaming inside my chest.

The house that we're at is on the small side, and that

says a lot since Ella and I both live in narrow, compact homes. It might only seem tiny, though, because there's a hundred plus sweaty drunk people pressed up together.

"I'm having fun!" Ella shouts breathlessly over the music. Her cheeks are flushed, her eyes are glazed over, and her smile lights up her entire face. The only time she ever looks this happy is either when we're at our spot near the lake or if she's drunk, like now.

"I'm glad. You deserve to have fun." My head slants to the side as she turns around to pour herself another drink with her good hand. My semi-intoxicated glaze leisurely glides up and down the lean curves of her body and linger on the black jeans she's wearing that hug her ass perfectly. Hug her *perfect* ass perfectly. *When did she get such a perfect ass?*

"Want me to pour you one?" She peers over her shoulder at me, then her expression sinks. "Hey! Were you just checking out my ass?"

I shrug, too drunk to conjure up a good lie. "It's nice to look at."

Her cheeks flush even more. "So gross, Micha," she

says, but by her blush, I wonder if she secretly might be thrilled.

I smirk at her. "Sure it is."

Shaking her head, she collects a plastic cup that she's filled to the brim with punch and vodka. She swallows a large gulp then faces me again, resting her hip against the counter as she stares at me.

"So, am I allowed to dance?" Ella asks, her gaze skimming around the throng, searching for options.

The idea of reliving the Jonny incident makes my fists clench. "You're allowed to do whatever you want," I reply through gritted teeth.

Her suffocating eyes land back on me. "You sound weird." She takes a sip from the cup, her gaze penetrating me from over the rim.

"You keep calling me weird." I lean in toward her, lowering my voice, forcing it to be playful. "It's starting to hurt my feelings, Ella May."

"Poor baby." She angles her head away from me and downs another swallow before setting the cup down on the countertop. "All right, if you're going to be weird about me

47

dancing, then I guess you'll just have to be my dance part-
ner." She laces her fingers through mine, alarming me so
badly I almost drop my cup on the floor.

Quickly recovering, I chuck it into a nearby trashcan
then tighten my hold on her hand as she steers me through
the mob. Ella and I have never danced before, but I know
how we both dance when we're drunk. Granted, Ella gets a
little skittish five minutes into the music, as if she suddenly
remembers something that leaves her wanting to be un-
touched. But if we make it through those five minutes ...

It's going to be the best fucking five minutes of my
life.

"You sure you want to do this?" She spins around as
we reach the center of the madness. There's hardly any
room, yet she somehow manages to spread her arms out
and shimmy her hips, raising her arms above her head and
giving me a full eyeful of her flat, smooth stomach.

Mother fucking hell.

I bite down on my lip to keep from moaning. If the
night keeps going in the same direction, I'm not going to be
able to keep my hands off her; otherwise, I'm going to ex-

plode.

Oblivious to the fact that her best friend is getting a hard on over her, Ella continues, "You know how intense I can get when I dance. I might embarrass Mr. Smooth." By her amused grin, I can tell she thinks she's teasing me. What she's really doing is adding fuel to the fire. She's totally fucking turning me on more than I ever have been before.

"Mr. Smooth?" I cock a brow at her. "Really?"

She shrugs as her hands fall to her sides. "Hey, you're the one who is always hitting on someone. I'm just giving you a fitting name."

I span my hands out to the side and glance around the crowd. "Do you see me hitting on anyone right now?"

The statement acutely puzzles her. "Now that you mention it, no." She leans in, squinting at my expression. "Are you sick or something?"

I roll my eyes. "I'm not as big of a manwhore as everyone thinks." When her brows elevate with insinuation, I shake my head and aim a finger at her. "You know what? This is for teasing me about my sluttiness." Before she can respond, I grab her hips and twirl her around so her back is to me. Then I quickly move up and align my body with hers. Moving to the rhythm of the throbbing music, I grind against her, knowing this can go either of two ways: she's going to think it's all for fun and move with me, or she's going to freak out and run.

She's tense as a board as the song ends and switches to "Ordinary World" by Red. Then, suddenly, Ella's dancing. *Ella and I* are dancing. I'm not even sure where the hell the burst of confidence materializes from, but she's now swaying and grinding and rocking to the slow beat of the song. And I'm instantly lost in her movements.

I'm so fucking lost.

Flirting has always come naturally to me, but I feel like a real amateur at the moment. I try to get a grip over myself, but as I start rubbing against her, I'm hyperaware of every breath, every graze of her ass, brush of her back, feel of her hands as they rise up and loop around the back of my neck. Our bodies align perfectly—too perfectly. They should always be together like this.

I'm struggling to control myself and not reach around

to slide my hand across her breasts, because I'm dying to touch her like that. Then her head falls to the side, giving me a straight view to her heaving chest, and my hands start to wander, take on a mind of their own, gliding around to the front of her and splaying across her stomach. My fingers play with the hem of her shirt, debating, before I summon up enough courage to slip them underneath the fabric.

God, her skin is so fucking smooth.

Her muscles tighten, and we both freeze.

She blinks up at me in confusion.

I stare down at her, my pulse pounding with desire, confusion, lust, heat, want, love, lust, love.

Then she starts to lean up.

Fuck, maybe she wants to kiss me.

I start to lean down.

Our lips inch closer.

We're about to kiss. Maybe my fear over my feelings was inaccurate. Perhaps I jumped to assumptions. Maybe she can handle my declaration of wanting more. Perhaps she does feel the same way about me as I do about her.

But just when a sliver of space is left between our lips, Ella's eyes snap wide. Reality painfully crashes over me.

"Oh, my God … Did we just …?" She trails off with a deer in the headlights look.

I open my mouth to say—well, who the fuck knows? Maybe something that could possibly make the situation even worse. Thankfully, Ella's friend Renee comes bouncing up to us and stops our conversation.

"What were you two just doing?" she asks with speculation, her gaze flicking back and forth between us.

"Nothing," Ella sputters, scooting forward and putting space between our bodies.

Leaving me feeling cold.

Renee assesses us closely. "Okay …" She shakes her head then focuses on Ella. "Well, anyway, I think you guys need to come have some fun with me." She grabs Ella's hand. "We're about to play truth or dare and need more players."

Ella throws a glance at me yet easily lets Renee drag her across the room with me trailing at their heels.

"Truth or dare?" Ella questions. "What are we, like

eight?"

Renee snorts a laugh. "Yeah, right, Ella. You're the biggest daredevil I know, so don't pretend like you don't love the idea."

Ella reaches back through the crowd as we squeeze toward the bedrooms and catches my hand. There's no clear reason as to why she does, but I don't care. I just grasp on for dear life.

"Who's playing?" Ella hollers over the music.

Renee releases Ella's hand as we reach a shut door at the back of the house near the kitchen. She brushes her chin-length hair out of her eyes then extends her hand for the doorknob. "Mara, Jonny, Grantford, Tammy..." Renee yammers off a list of people.

Ella makes a face at the mention of Tammy, shooting a dirty look at me, probably because I hooked up with Tammy a couple of weeks ago. I'd be offended, but I think I might detect a slight bit of jealousy in her eyes so I'm more elated than anything.

Renee opens the door and we enter a room that has zero furniture inside it. The only thing occupying the shaggy orange carpet are the people Renee yammered off along with a few others I don't know and my friend Ethan Gregory.

Ethan starts to give me a chin nod, but then his gaze darts to Ella's and my hands clasped together. As his brow arches in perplexity, I shrug. I might be kind of slutty, but I've never gone around holding a girl's hand; I've never had a girlfriend, just hookups. Right now, I'm sure Ella and I look like a couple, but that's more than fine with me.

"Okay, Ella." Renee nudges Ella in Grantford's direction and our hands slip apart. "You take a seat over there." Then she shoves me in the opposite direct. "Micha, you go sit by Tammy."

As I look over at Tammy, who's batting her eyelashes at me, I realize that not only is everyone sitting in a circle, but there's also an empty beer bottle in the center of them.

"Wait." I glance back at Renee. "I thought you said we were playing truth or dare?"

"Did I?" She thrums a finger on her lips. "You must have misheard me."

Fucking Renee. She's always lying and tricking people

into doing shit. Although, I have the slightest bit of suspicion that Tammy played a part in this. Ever since I hooked up with her, she's been following me around at school, asking me when we're going to get together again.

Blowing out a frustrated breath, I plop my ass down in the empty spot next to Tammy. Ella has already sat down by Grantford, who gawks at her chest when she rests back on her hands and crisscrosses her legs. She appears a little dazed, lost in her thoughts as she stares at the bare walls and closet door of the room.

Even when the game gets going, Ella remains oddly out of it. I half expect her to leave at any moment, not because we're playing spin the bottle, but because Ella's the kind of person that will get riled up over the fact that Renee lied about the game. Instead, she twirls a strand of her hair around her finger, oblivious when Ethan kisses Mara.

Then Grantford takes a turn, and it's clear he has his sights set on Ella, yet he gets stuck kissing someone else. She doesn't even notice when Jonny spins and the bottle lands on Ethan, causing Ethan to get all squirrely and Jonny to take another turn. The only time she actually focuses on what's going on is when Tammy gives the bottle a spin and bounces up and down excitedly when the tip points at me.

"Yes! I get Micha." She grins at me as she gets up and turns toward me, wiggling her hips.

When I glance over at Ella, her expression is unreadable, although there's something in her eyes that I've never seen before, something that makes my adrenaline pump a little faster. The longer we stare at each other, the more intense the sensation grows. While Ella knows I hook up, she's never actually seen me kiss anyone, and I think the idea is bothering her.

"Micha, I'm over here." Tammy snaps her fingers in front of my face. I tear my attention away from Ella and look up at Tammy. Her hands are on her hips and her eyes are flooded with irritation. "You're supposed to be kissing me," she says hotly then wets her lips with her tongue.

"Kissing ... yeah. Okay." I stand up and plant probably the quickest, tongueless, sloppiest kiss in history. Then I swing around her and move to the bottle in the middle of the circle.

"What the hell, Micha?" Tammy seethes from behind

me. "That so didn't even count."

Ignoring her protests and Renee's scowls, I wrap my fingers around the glass bottle. I've played it enough that I'm fairly confident I can pull off what I'm about to do. What I'm not confident in is how Ella is going to handle.

Still, I do it.

I spin the bottle with just enough force that it goes around the circle one time and a little over, landing right on Ella.

Her eyes widen as it points to her then her gaze cuts to me. Her lips part to protest, but I quickly shrug like *what are you going to do?* Then I kneel down on the carpet in front of her, noting how excited I am to kiss her, like I was at fourteen. I never get this excited for a kiss. *Ever.* Ella's got me two for two.

"It won't hurt. I promise," I feel the need to say as I lean into her because she looks absolutely horrified. Maybe I should back off. Not be so selfish. Walk away because this might be too much for her to handle.

But I want it. Badly. Want her. Even in front of a room full of people who are gawking at us like they're about to watch a porno.

"Micha," she whispers as I dip my lips toward hers. "I think …" She trails off as I move in closer, her chest ravenously heaving as she struggles for oxygen. Her hands come up, her fingers folding around my arms, her nails piercing into my flesh. The heat of our breaths mixes as our lips inch closer.

When only a whisper of air is left, she lets out the softest whimper that nearly sends me soaring through the roof. I place a hand on each side of her, pinning her between my arms, my fingers gripping at the carpet for support. Fuck, I haven't even touched her yet, and my body feels like it's going to combust.

Back away.

Don't do it.

Stop …

Oh, my God …

Our lips connect and her hold on me constricts, begs for me to keep her together. I want to, but I feel like I'm about to collapse myself. Because, just like that, I'm kissing my best friend. I'm kissing my best friend who I'm in love with and who might not love me back—at least, not in the same way. But I don't care. I want to do more. I want to kiss her while laying her back and spreading open her legs so I can grind my hips against her like we were doing on the dance floor only a half an hour ago.

There's not even any tongue to the kiss, yet it's consuming, savoring, heart stopping. It's a kiss I wish would last forever, but as quick as it started, it ends as Ella springs back.

"God dammit, Micha," she curses as she turns and trips to her feet. Then she bolts out of the room, slamming the door behind her.

"Jesus, what a freak," Tammy mutters. When I glare at her, she narrows her eyes at me. "What? She is."

Shaking my head, I chase after Ella, disregarding Ethan's protest to just let her cool off. By the time I make it to the living room, the crowd has doubled, and the air is so stuffy I can barely breathe. Still, I search for her in the sea of bodies, needing to find her, to fix this.

But how exactly are you going to do that?

After doing countless laps around the house, I finally

stop inside the kitchen, getting discouraged. "Fuck!" I growl. Finding Ella is going to be nearly impossible with this many people around.

Pissed off at myself, I shove through the people, heading for the back door so I can go outside and smoke. Maybe a little fresh air and nicotine will clear my head. When I step out the door, though, I find exactly what I was looking for.

Ella is sitting on the icy bottom stair of the porch with a cup in her hand with her jacket off and goose bumps dot her flesh. For a brief moment, I stand at the top of the stairway, staring at her, trying to figure out what the heck to say. I'm sorry? Yeah, I don't think so. I'm the opposite of sorry. That kiss made me realize just how much I was missing out on—behind the connection of lips, there's supposed to be emotion, passion, heat, and intensity instead of boredom.

"What are you doing out here without a jacket." I sink down beside her and reach for the zipper on my hoodie. "You're going to freeze to death."

Her body jolts from my appearance, and she drops her

cup. Clear liquid spills across the snow as it rolls down the steps and into driveway. Her eyelashes flutter furiously as her gaze locks on me.

"What are you doing out here?" she asks, her breath reeking of vodka.

Jesus, what did she do, drink a whole damn bottle in the twenty minutes it took me to find her?

"I'm saving your ass from freezing." I shuck off my jacket and drape it over her shoulders.

"I'm not cold." It takes her a moment before she stubbornly gives in and slips her arms through the sleeves. Then she lowers her head into her hands. "Why did you do that?"

"Do what?" I ask, even though I know exactly what she's talking about.

She scowls at me. "You know what. Make that bottle purposefully land on me."

"You know me better than I thought," I respond, searching her eyes for an indication that I haven't fucked up our friendship. But she's indecipherable. "Was it really that bad, though?"

"Depends on why you did it." Her voice wobbles the slightest bit.

I shrug, stretching my legs out as I stare up at the stars. "Out of curiosity, I guess."

"Curiosity of what?" She lifts her head. "We've already done the whole curious kissing thing. Why do we need to do it again?"

I rub my chilled arms. "Maybe I just wanted to see if things had changed." *If my feelings had changed. My feelings for you. And they have. They really, really have. More than I realized.*

"Micha, I …" Her breath puffs out in a cloud in front of her face as she begins to panic. "Please, just say you did it for fun, and it didn't mean anything," she whispers, pleads, begs. "Because I can't handle anything else."

My heart breaks.

Shatters.

Scatters across the ground.

Like fragments of ice.

"Well, you know me." My voice is dry, humorless as I stare at the ground. "I'm all about the joking and random kisses." When I'm finally able to look at her again, I come to an excruciating realization. Even though the kiss happened, it can't ever really happen. Ella and I can't really become anything more than what we are, not right now, anyway. Ella is relying on me to say so; otherwise, she's going to break apart. And, if I really do love her, I'll do everything in my power to keep her together like I've been doing for the last twelve years.

"I didn't want it to land on Tammy." I swallow hard, aware that this might be the first lie I've ever told Ella. "And Ethan has a thing for Mara. Plus, there was no fucking way I was going to kiss Renee." I causally shrug, even though my insides are wound tight. "You were my safest option."

She relaxes a little.

And I die a bit inside.

"I'm so glad to hear you say that. For a minute there, I thought ..." She quickly shakes her head. "It was weird, right? The kiss."

All I can do is nod.

"You know what we should do." She spits on her hand

and my heart withers inside my chest even more. "We should make a pact to never, ever kiss again."

I can't make that pact.

I grind my teeth as I stare at her hand. "I have a better idea. How about we make a pact never to speak of this kiss again." It's the only way I can think of to get around this.

She considers what I've said then nods. "Okay, that sounds good to me."

I spit in my hand, then we shake on it. Part of me is saddened that I'll never get to speak of this night again because that kiss was the kind of kiss I want to relive over and over again, even if it's through words. But the other part of me is relieved because I don't want to relive the pain I'm feeling right now, over and over again.

The pain of heart break.

The only thing that keeps me from breaking down is the fact that I tell myself things could change. Ella and I have years to spend together, and in time, her fear of commitment could change.

It has to change.

Chapter 3

Seventeen years old...

Ella

I can sense trouble coming from a mile away. Why? Because I'm exhausted, and that usually leads to trouble. It's been a long week. Summer is nearing an end. My dad's working less, so there's hardly any money to pay bills and buy food. Dean is gone and that leaves me to take care of the household. And my mom's having one of her rough days today. It's Saturday, and I spent the entire afternoon searching for a photo of when our family took a trip to the sandy beaches of California, even though the photo doesn't exist. But I have to look for it until my mom is satisfied that it's lost; otherwise, she'll continue to have a panic attack until she has a meltdown.

"Ella, please find it," she begs as she follows me into the small, disordered living room, tugging at the roots of her reddish-brown hair. Her eyes are enlarged, her pupils dilated. I'm starting to worry she might have snuck an extra dose of her medication again.

"I'm trying to find it, Mom." I lift up the couch cushions and check underneath them before I rummage around inside a few boxes stacked by the front door. "I think it might be gone, though."

"I have to find it, Ella." Her voice trembles as she starts to pace the length of the room, maneuvering around the ashtrays, beer bottles, and my dad who's passed out drunk on the floor in front of the television. "Please, I need to remember what happened that day. It was a good day. I know it was. I know they exist."

"They do exist," I play along, unsure if it's the right thing to do or not, but I've spent enough time with her that I know she'll calm down eventually. "And that day was a really, really good day. I promise."

"How do you know for sure?" She stops in the middle of the room and crosses her arms, her eyes skimming the boxes, walls, and windows.

"Because ..." Sighing heavily, I wind around the coffee table and move in front of her to keep her focused on me. "Because I remember going, and I remember Dad, Dean, and I saying that we had a great time with you."

She rocks back and forth, hugging her arms tighter around herself. "Good, but ... I can't remember it. Please, help me remember, Ella."

"Well, it was a really sunny and warm day. The air smelled like salt and water and all the scents of the ocean ... We spent all afternoon collecting seashells and building sand castles." As I create a story for her, I find myself wishing it was real. My family hasn't taken many trips, but it would have been nice to, if only once, go somewhere for fun, like an amusement park, or hell, I'll take just a park at this point. The only place I can recollect going for a vacation was to the zoo back when I was six and money and life wasn't as bad as they are now. It was a time when there was less yelling, and my mother's delusions and manic depressive episodes hadn't manifested.

A minute later, my mother starts to settle down, her arms relaxing at her sides while her posture slackens. "Did we have a picnic near the shore? Because I remember having one."

I nod, relaxing myself. "Yeah, we had one right there on the beach, and we ate under this really large, yellow umbrella."

"Oh, it sounds like we had fun." She almost smiles.

So do I. "We did."

"Good, I'm glad." She pauses, rubbing her hands up and down her arms like she's cold, even though it's the nearly eighty degrees outside. "You know what? I think I flew that day, too, like I did at the bridge."

I swallow hard. My mother's obsession with flying has been growing worse over the years. Whenever she gets stuck inside her own head, she insists she can fly. There was one day not too long ago when she left the house, and I found her on the old town bridge, trying to actually fly. It was one of the most terrifying days of my life, and it was also the day I realized just how severe my mother's condition is. If I hadn't showed up when I did ... Well, I don't like to think about it too much.

As her eyelids start to lower, I know she's veering toward the energy crash she always has after a panic attack. "Baby girl," she says, dragging her feet toward the stairs,

"I'm going to go take a nap, just for a little while. I'll be back in a bit."

"Okay." I follow her up the stairs anyway, just to make sure she gets there. Then I help her get into bed and pull the covers over her.

"I'm pretty sure I can fly, Ella May," she whispers right before she passes out.

After I tuck her in, I pick up the dirty dishes and food wrappers on the dresser, cleaning up. By the time I walk out of her room, she's fast asleep.

Relief washes over me as I shut the door behind me. I feel a pang of guilt over being glad she fell asleep, but deep down, I know it's a good thing because I'm tired, and eventually, I would have snapped at her and made the situation worse.

I wander downstairs to put the garbage in the kitchen trash can and clean off the plates. Then I pick up the collection of alcohol bottles and put them in the trash bin. I sort through the bills, making a past due pile and a 'can be put on hold for a little while' pile before dragging my ass to my room and collapsing onto my bed. The house is quiet. Still.

And I feel completely alone. I always do whenever I'm home.

As my eyelids drift shut, I think of another place, another world, another life where my only concern is school, myself, and what I'm going to do on Saturday night.

Stretching my arms out, I reach beneath my pillow and let my fingers brush against the envelope I hid there a couple of months ago, right before graduation. It's the one piece of mail I was actually happy to receive—my admissions letter to the University of Las Vegas. Quite honestly, I was surprised when I got accepted. Although, the financial aid I received wasn't that big of a shock. Still, the money doesn't cover the cost of everything. But I have some saved up from a few part time jobs I've had here and there. Once I get down there, I'll get a job and work my ass off to survive. I want to—want that ticket out of here. I'm still not sure if I can do it, though. Bail out on my mom. Leave her behind with only my alcoholic father to take care of her. And then, of course, there's Micha.

Micha and our pact to leave this town together.

I haven't worked up the courage to tell him that I even

applied to colleges, let alone that I got into one that's over twelve hours away.

What the hell am I going to do? How am I going to tell everyone? How can I just leave all of my responsibilities behind?

Sighing heavily, I bury my face in my pillow and briefly consider not coming up for air again. Maybe I'll just stop breathing. Giving up would be simpler. Letting go. Saying an eternal good-bye instead of facing the tough choices ahead of me, whether I stay here or decide to go to Vegas.

Ultimately, when my face becomes too hot and my lungs ache from lack of oxygen, I flip over to my side and suck in a deep inhale. Then I glance at the alarm clock on my nightstand. Six thirty-seven. Shit! I was supposed to meet Micha at six. Hopefully he hasn't left, because I was really looking forward to getting out of the house today.

I start to push up from my bed, but a second later, my window creaks open and sunlight filters through the room.

"What are you, like seventy?" Micha jokes as his boots thud against the floor.

"What are you, a creepy pervert?" I retort, rolling over

and pressing my cheek against the mattress, while fighting back a smile. "Creeping into my room like a weirdo."

"Yep. And damn proud of it," he says cockily. Moments later, the mattress concaves as he climbs onto my bed and nuzzles up against me, aligning his chest and hips to my back and butt. "What are you doing in bed?"

"Sleeping," I murmur, snuggling into his body heat. "Can't you tell?"

"And sleep talking apparently." He chuckles as his fingers slide up the back of my bare thigh and pinch my ass cheek that's peeking out of my denim shorts.

"What the hell, Micha!" I squeal, flipping over to my side to glare at him.

He's sporting a black T-shirt with a green logo on it, dark jeans secured with a studded belt, and boots with the laces untied. The look is topped off with his classic *I'm so charming* grin.

"That's for calling me a creepy pervert," he says. "If you're going to call me one, then I'm going to act like one."

"But you're a pervert all the time," I point out. It's the

truth, too. He only gets away with it because he's cute and charming.

His aqua eyes darken as his fingers curl around the curve of my hip. "Call me that again, and I'm going to show you just how perverted I am."

Ignoring the stupid flutter in my stomach, I roll my eyes and pinch his arm. His eyes crinkle around the corners as he laughs.

As his laughter silences, he rakes his sandy blonde hair out of his eyes and stares down at me. "So, I know we were supposed to go to the party tonight, but I was thinking maybe we could go racing instead?" He traces a line down my cheekbone with his finger while nibbling on the silver ring ornamenting his bottom lip.

The stupid flutter in my stomach emerges again and panic soars through me. Like always, I'm not even sure what to make of the damn sensation. It's been manifesting a lot lately, especially when Micha touches me or sucks on that lip ring of his. I find the flutter a bit revolting. Unwelcomed. Exciting. Terrifying. Confusing. Too many things, honestly.

Micha arches a brow at me. "What's wrong?"

I realize how profusely I'm breathing while staring at his lips like a creeper myself.

Blinking out of my daze and composing my erratic breathing, I roll over onto my back to put some space between us. "I'm not sure I feel up for racing tonight." I stare up at my ceiling, trying not to pout. As much as I love racing, I am eager to let loose at the party and dance and drink until my body and mind are numb.

"Pretty please?" he begs, lowering his tone to a soft purr, using *the voice* on me. The damn flutters drive me crazy again. "It will be my first time racing since the accident, and I want you to be there with me to hold my hand."

I snort a laugh as I turn my head to look at him. "What are we, in kindergarten again?"

His pout deepens. "Please?"

"Micha, you don't need me. I promise, you'll be okay by yourself."

His mouth plummets to a frown. "I always need you."

I sigh, feeling even guiltier about the letter hiding under the pillow right beneath my head. "I thought your car

74

wasn't ready to race yet."

He absentmindedly reaches across me and twists a lock of my auburn hair around his finger. "No, Ethan and I got all the shit that was broken taken care of, so I'm good to go." He springs up and grabs my hands, tugging on my arms until I sit up. "Now get your ass out of bed and come with me. You know I can't win without you."

I roll my eyes and dramatically let my head bobble back. "That is so not true. You've won plenty of times without me."

He melodramatically presses his hand to his heart while still holding onto one of my wrists. "It's completely true. I'd lose without you, baby."

I give an over-exaggerated gag, wiggling my arm away from his grasp to place my fingers at the base of my neck. "Have you been reading the *Cheesy Pickup Lines Handbook* again? Because I thought I forbid you to do that anymore." It's amazing, but the pressure in my chest is lighter. Even when I was younger, I felt like a completely different person when I was around Micha: stronger, happier, weightless, like anything was possible. Which makes leaving to Vegas without him terrifying.

"Yeah, but I already got it memorized." He backs off the bed and stands up. Then he winks at me. "Come on, pretty girl, go with me."

I point a finger at him. "Watch the nickname, mister. You know I don't like being called that."

His lips quirk as he restrains a smile. "I'll stop calling you that for tonight if you promise to go with me."

There's no use arguing with him. He pretty much won the argument the moment he started it. I always give in and go with him because he'll make me feel fifty times better, even with the crowd of people around us. Besides, I'm craving the freedom from my house, and I need to take what I can get.

"Is ditzy going to be there tonight?" I ask, swinging my legs over the edge of the bed and lowering my feet to the floor.

"You mean Trixie?" he corrects me, amused. "Why? Will you be jealous if she is?"

I scrunch up my nose. "Don't flatter yourself."

Trixie was Micha's weekend hook up last Saturday.

While I'm used to his random flings since he's been doing them for a couple of years now, it still irritates me. Even though I will never admit it aloud, I want Micha all to myself, as selfish as it seems. He's all I have, and … Well, I feel lost without him.

"You sure about that? Because you seemed pretty bitchy toward Trixie the other day." He arches his eyebrow, which pisses me off. It seems like he's insinuating something that I don't like. And that isn't true at all.

Well, maybe …

I'm not sure.

God, I'm not sure about anything anymore when it comes to him.

"Yeah, I'm sure." I extend my hand forward and pinch his nipple through his shirt. "One of these days, that head of yours is going to get so big you aren't going to be able to fit it through my window anymore."

He chuckles as he rubs his nipple. "You better watch it, or one of these days, I'm going to pinch you right back."

I quickly cross my arms over my chest because I don't doubt that he will. "Okay, here's the deal. I'll go with you, but only if you stop with the dirty jokes, calling me pretty girl, and come home with me. And we have to at least stop by the party on our way there."

"I agree to the latter three, but the first one is completely out of my hands." He grins as he points to his mouth. "This thing doesn't have a filter."

"Fine," I surrender. "Just try to tone it down, if you can."

Nodding, he leans forward to kiss my cheek. "Thank you for going with me, pretty ... beautiful," he whispers, his breath hot against my skin.

Flutters. Flutters. Flutters.

I struggle back the urge to shiver as he stands up straight and backs toward the window. "Meet me downstairs after you change."

My forehead creases. "Why would I change? What I'm wearing is perfectly fine."

He bites on his bottom lip so hard the skin around his mouth turns white. Then his gaze flicks to my chest. "Well, you don't *have* to change, but you might want to consider it." He rubs his hand across his mouth, dragging his fingers roughly across his skin, as if he's stressed out. "Or at least consider putting on ... a bra before you come out." He quickly turns his back to me and swings his leg out the window to climb out.

My gaze drifts to my chest and my eyes widen. I completely forgot that this morning, when my mom woke me up freaking out about the photo, I just tugged on the nearest thing and didn't bother putting on a bra. Right now, with the lightest breeze in my room, my nipples are perky and can be seen through the fabric of my shirt. They've probably been that way the entire time Micha and I were talking.

I hear Micha bust up laughing the moment he escapes my room and makes it out onto the tree branch. With one arm crossed over my chest, I hop off the bed, pick up a pillow, and stride across the room toward the window. I chuck the pillow out at him, and it hits him square in the back then tumbles to the grass below. Micha laughs even harder as he turns around and places his hands on the windowsill, ducking his head in to look at me.

"You're cute when you're embarrassed," he says with a grin.

Keeping my arm over my chest, I narrow my eyes at him. "I'm not embarrassed."

"Your pink cheeks suggest otherwise." He sucks on his lip ring, and I prepare myself for the innuendo coming. "You don't need to be embarrassed. What I saw was nice. Way better than any I've seen before."

My lips part in shock.

"And I think that you secretly kind of like that I was looking," he adds arrogantly. "Otherwise, you would have punched me in the face already, like you do to any other guy who comments on your tits."

My jaw is practically hanging to my knees. Before I can offer a rebuttal, he winks at me then hurries away from the window, balancing on the tree branch with his arms out.

"You're such an ass," I call out after him. "I don't like that you were looking. At all." The butterflies in my stomach reveal differently, though.

"Whatever you have to tell yourself to get you through the day." He flashes me one final grin before he descends down the tree.

Blowing out a frustrated breath, I return to my bed and

flop down on the mattress, angry at myself because Micha's right. If any other guy had said what he just did, I would have clocked him square in the jaw. But, with Micha … Part of me secretly enjoys our sexual banter, something we've done since we hit our early teens, and he started noticing I had breasts. Still, it's just friendly, flirty fun that I know will never go anywhere. Nor do I want him to want me as more than friends. Crossing that line would mean losing our friendship, and I can't lose Micha. *Ever.* Besides, I'm not emotionally ready to be committed to a guy, which is why I've never had a boyfriend. A few make out sessions, yeah. But nothing past second base. I just don't get the whole touching thing. Hugs. Kisses. Fondling. Whatever. It freaks me out more than it turns me on. The only person I've ever felt comfortable touching me is Micha.

Two minutes later, I drag my ass out of bed and put a bra on beneath my white tank top. Then I tug my leather jacket on, even though it's hot, just so I can have peace of mind that I won't nipple flash anyone for the rest of the night. I pull my auburn hair into a ponytail, trace my green eyes with some kohl eyeliner, and slip on black combat boots before heading downstairs.

When I turn into the kitchen, my dad is awake, rummaging through his alcohol stash in the cupboard above the fridge. His thinning hair is in disarray, his plaid jacket and dirty jeans reeking of liquor and cigarette smoke.

"Have you seen my bottle of Jack Daniels?" he asks me, his speech slurred as he staggers to keep his footing. He ends up tripping over his shoelace and bangs his head against the corner of the cupboard. "Shit," he curses, rubbing his head. "That kind of hurt."

I almost turn around and leave, walk out the front door and ignore the problem. Bur leaving him starving for alcohol is never a good idea.

"Let me see if I can find it," I tell him, gently nudging him out of the way as I move up to the counter. Seconds later, I find the bottle right there on the middle shelf amongst the rest of his alcohol stash. "Here you go." I hand it to him, feeling a bit guilty for being an aid to his addiction. But I also know what will happen if I don't give it to him: madness; chaos; and a lot of yelling, crying, and broken things for me to clean up in the morning.

He snatches the bottle from my hand and swishes it around, eyeballing the amber liquid through the glass. "It's almost gone," he mutters. "Go pick up some more for me."

"The gas station won't let me buy anymore," I tell him, ready to get the hell out of the house for the damn night. "The guy who sold alcohol to minors got busted, and he doesn't work there anymore."

"That's stupid. What the hell am I going to do now?" he gripes, glaring at the bottle in his hand.

"You could stay sober for the weekend," I timidly suggest. "It might help with the hangover on Monday."

When he glares at me with his bloodshot eyes, I shrink back.

"Fine." He slams the bottle down on the table. "I'll go get it myself."

"Dad, I don't think you should go out by yourself when you're like this."

He waves me off as he zips up his jacket, oblivious to the heat outside. "I'll be back in five. Keep an eye on your mother."

"Dad, I'm leav—"

He walks out of the house, slamming the door.

I let out a deflated sigh then text Micha.

Me: Going to be a bit. Dad needed to go somewhere.

Micha: Ok, I'll wait for u.

Me: U don't have to ... U should just go without me.

Micha: Don't want to. Never do.

Part of me smiles, desiring the escape he'll give me no matter how selfish it is to make him wait for me.

Me: Fine. See c in a bit.

I tuck my phone in my pocket and recline against the counter, watching the back door for my dad to return. Thirty minutes tick by, and I sink down in the kitchen chair. I rotate a bottle of vodka in my hand as I watch the sun descend outside the window and grey the land. Waiting. Waiting. Waiting.

An hour later, I take a swallow of the vodka, growing restless. I can't even text my dad to see where he is, because he lost his cell phone one drunken night, and we can't afford a new one.

I end up finishing the vodka off. There was only about three shots in there, but since I don't drink very much, I can feel the dizziness swishing around inside me. My phone buzzes, and I check the message, squinting against the glow of the screen.

Micha: Where r u?

Me: Dad's still gone. I'm on mom duty.

Micha: U want me to come over?

I consider texting yes, but I really want to go out tonight, so I send a different reply.

Me: Give me 10 and I'll be over.

Then I push back from the table and check on my mom. She's still fast asleep in her bed, and knowing her past routines, she should stay that way until morning. Even though I feel the slightest bit guilty, I put her cell phone on the nightstand beside the bed. Then I trot down the stairway and leave the house.

It'll be okay. I'll only stay out for a few hours. And my dad will be back.

Besides, maybe tonight will finally be the night I'll

muster up the courage to tell Micha that I might have to break our pact.

Chapter 4

Micha

Ella's had a rough day. That's the first thing I noted when I climbed into the window and heard her voice. Then she rolled over in her bed, and the next thing that popped into my head was, *Jesus, I can see her nipples through her shirt.* She must have been cold, too, because they were perky as hell. I both love and hate how fucking hot she is. It leaves me with a hard on that I can't do much about except for jerk off, which is exactly what I did when I got home.

If I had my way, I would've ripped Ella's clothes off and slipped deep inside her. But she's like a skittish cat when it comes to connection, contact, and her emotions. She's been a little better about it the older she's gotten, though not with everyone. As much as I loathe that her emotionally numb, selfish parents have made her so non-reciprocating to affection, part of me secretly likes that I'm the only one who gets away with touching her, like the ass pinch earlier.

About an hour after hopping out Ella's window, I'm in the garage, fiddling around with the engine of my 1969 Chevelle, waiting for her to show up. The Beast, as I call it, is a real piece of shit yet was way worse when I first towed it home. At least it has wheels now and bondo concealing the dents, and most of the exterior metal is a dull grey from the primer. It still needs a lot of work, like a paint job and new rims, but the engine runs fucking fantastic.

I pass the time as I check the oil and antifreeze, making sure it's ready to go for tonight's race. The radio is playing, and I sing along to the lyrics of "Imperfect" by Stone Sour.

The sky eventually starts to grey with the sunset, and I try not to worry about how late it's getting and that Ella is still a no show. It means whatever is going on in her house is bad. That's usually the case. Either her mother is having an episode, or her father is trashed and being a huge dick.

"I thought you said it was good to race." Ella suddenly appears beside me.

Startled, I jerk back, banging my head on the hood.

"Shit," I curse, rubbing my head.

Ella smashes her lips together, trying not to laugh at me. "Are you okay?"

"I'm fine." I toss the rag I'm holding onto the shelf behind me while discreetly checking out Ella as she leans over to examine the engine.

Her tight cutoff shorts hug her perfect ass, her combat boots are laced up to her knees, and she has her favorite leather jacket on that makes her look sexy as hell. But what really causes my heart to beat like a fucking jackhammer is those big green eyes of hers.

Those gorgeous eyes that are swallowing me up whole right now.

"Why are you staring at me like that?" Ella asks, self-consciously touching a strand of her hair. "Is there something in my hair?"

I shake my head, unable to take my eyes off her. "Nope, you look perfect as always."

She narrows her eyes at me as her head falls to the side. "Nice try. I look like crap right now."

"You're welcome for the compliment." I smirk at her,

glad I can veer toward joking territory because it's all I can take anymore. Things used to be less complicated when something as simple as her scent didn't send my senses off into a mad frenzy. Now, I'm pretty much holding my breath every time I'm near her. And I'm near her a lot, so things are constantly intense.

Some of her tension alleviates, her shoulders unwinding. "Sorry. I'm being kind of a bitch, aren't I?"

"A little. But I'm sure you have your reasons." I pause, knowing it'll do no good, but I have to ask—have to try. "Want to talk about whatever's bothering you?"

She swiftly shakes her head then moves up to me and loops her arms around the back of my neck. "I just want to have fun. Can we do that?"

My breath catches in my throat from her nearness. I'm seriously about to pour my heart out to her right here in my garage. But I detect the slightest scent of alcohol on her breath and stop myself from doing the irreversible.

I frown. "You're drunk."

"Yeah, so?" She stares up at me with a challenge in her eyes. "You get drunk all the time."

"Yeah, but you only get drunk when something's bothering you." I glance at her house next door. The lights are off except for the porch light, and her dad's Firebird is parked in the driveway. "Was it your mom or dad this time?"

"It's nothing. No one did anything."

"Ella May," I warn, "I know when you're lying."

She sighs as she steps away from me with her shoulders hunched. "My dad went out for alcohol over an hour ago and left me in charge of my mom. He was only supposed to be gone for like five minutes, but you know how that goes."

I rest my palm against her cheek, fighting a smile when she embraces my touch, knowing it'd be an inappropriate reaction right now. "I'll stay home with you tonight, okay? We'll just chill at your house and keep an eye on your mother."

"No. I'm not going to let you do that … give up any more fun for me."

"You and I are in this together, remember? It's you and me against the world. Besides, whether we go out or stay in doesn't matter. As long as I'm with you." I know how cheesy I sound, and she's more than likely going to give me shit for it. I can't help it, though. Stuff like that just falls out of my mouth whenever I'm around her.

Her lips quirk, but then her expression plunges and laces with apprehension. She moves her face away from my hand. "Micha, there's something I need to talk to you about."

"Okay." I'm becoming nervous myself, wondering what the hell could be causing her to look so anxious.

"It's about our future plans." She summons a deep breath. "I know we were supposed to hit the road soon, but I ..." She trails off, her gaze wandering to her house where her dad is stumbling up the driveway, cursing under his breath.

He has a brown paper bag in his hand, and he keeps stopping to take swings from it. I'm honestly surprised he can walk with how out of it he looks.

"Just let him go," I tell Ella. With as drunk as her father is, he's more than likely going to upset her more tonight.

"I have to see if he's okay." Ella rounds the back of my car and exits the garage. "Dad, where have you been?" Ella calls out as she walks up to the fence dividing our properties.

He blinks around until he finally spots her then staggers to a sloppy halt. "What? Who are you …? Oh, Ella, is that you?"

"Yeah, um …" She glances back at me. I already know what's coming before she even says it. "Micha, I think I need to stay home tonight to take care of my mom and dad. You just go, okay?"

I move up beside her. "I already told you I'm not going out without you."

"What the hell is your problem?" Her dad shouts over me, tripping backwards until his back hits the side of the house. "Why aren't you in the house?"

Ella clutches the top of the fence until her knuckles turn white. "Dad, you aren't—"

"Shut up!" he screams so loudly the neighbor's dog starts howling. "You stupid little bitch!"

My blood boils. I swear to God, I want to punch the

asshole in the face. Every fucking time he gets this drunk, this shit happens. And Ella always looks like a wounded dog, ready to curl up in a ball. The girl can fight like no other with everyone else, but put her in front of her verbally abusive dad, and she shuts down.

It fucking hurts to watch her die inside.

"Fuck off, Mr. Daniels!" I snap, enraged. "You're drunk, and you need to go inside before you say anything else you'll regret." Like the fucking douche ever regrets anything. He's never sober long enough to feel regret.

"All I regret is having this family," he slurs, flinging his arm at us as he stumbles for the back stairs and lands on his ass. "You and your little shit brother ruined my life."

I hold my breath and stab my nails into my palms until he gets to his feet and stumbles back down the driveway, probably heading to the bar again, a typical Saturday night for him.

"I'll be back in a bit!" he shouts as he zigzags across the front lawn.

Once he's vanished down the sidewalk, I let out a deafening breath. Then, with one more inhale, I face Ella.

She hasn't spoken a word since her father yelled at her, and her eyes are glued to the ground.

"Are you okay?" I ask, daring to place my hand on the small of her back.

She stiffens from my touch yet doesn't move away. "I should stay and keep an eye on stuff ..." She releases a loud breath and then finally looks up at me. "You know what? Never mind. I'm going to go with you tonight and have some fun. My mother has her cell phone. I just have to make sure I check up on her. Although, I doubt she'll be awake tonight. The meds she's on are pretty heavy."

"Are you sure? Because I don't mind—"

She conceals my mouth with her hand. "Nope, you and I are going out tonight. No buts."

"Yes, boss." Then, just because I know it'll make her smile, I lick the palm of her hand.

"Micha!" she squeals, laughing as she backs away, bumping her hip against the fence. "That's so gross."

I artfully grin. "My tongue's been inside your mouth before. How could that be any grosser?"

She puts her hands on her hips. "Hey, who said I didn't

think the kiss was gross?"

"My kisses aren't gross," I assure her.

"At fourteen, maybe they were."

I mock being offended, pressing a hand to my chest like she's wounded my heart. Really, she has the complete power to do so. "Wow, way to ruin my ego. For four years, I thought I rocked your world, and now you're telling me I didn't."

She flashes me a haughty smile. "No way. I've had way better kisses." She whirls around, and I watch her ass as she saunters over to my car.

"That's such bullshit." I chase after her, no longer pretending I'm offended anymore—I *am* offended. That kiss rocked my fucking world. Hell, it might have been the starting point of the obsession I've developed for her.

When I reach her, I dodge around and barricade her path to the passenger side of the car. "That kiss was the best you've ever had. Admit it."

She crosses her arms, giving me a glimpse of my very favorite side of her—the bold, spitfire side. "So you want me to lie to you?"

"Wow," I say sullenly, massaging my aching chest with my balled fist. "That fucking hurts, Ella. You seriously just broke my heart."

"What can I say?" She puts her lips close to my face, eliciting a stutter from my aching heart. "Payback's a bitch," she whispers then licks my neck, giggling under her breath as she steps back, totally proud of herself. "That was for the hand lick." She smirks then veers around me to get into the Chevelle, leaving me speechless.

And fucking rock hard.

I adjust my cock then take about one more minute to compose myself before slamming the hood of the car down and climbing in the driver's seat. Then I rev up the engine, telling myself not to ask, but my need to know overcomes me.

"So, was the payback just the lick?" I rotate in my seat to look at her. "Or was the remark about the kiss part of your evil, heart breaking plan, too?"

Her green eyes sparkle with amusement. "What do you think?"

"I think it was a great fucking kiss, especially for being

only fourteen." I drape my arm on the seat behind her head and play with her hair. "But I want to know what you think."

She slumps her head against the seat, chewing on her bottom lip as she struggles with something internally, her playful mood shifting. "I think the kiss was ... great," she whispers softly. "You're great, Micha." With that, she turns away from me and stares out the window.

"You're great, too." *And I love you. I'm* in *love with you, Ella.*

My tongue burns to utter the last words, the thing I've wanted to tell her for almost two years now, but like always, I chicken out. I can't have my relationship with Ella end. Can't—won't—live my life without her. And, if it means we have to stay friends, then we have to stay friends. I just hope, with time, she'll finally be able to feel the same way toward me. Maybe when we get out of this shitty town and start our life together, like we've been planning since age fourteen.

Burying my emotions, I instead say exactly what she needs to hear. "You ready for some fun tonight?" I pump the gas pedal and the engine roars to life.

Her attention whips back to me. She attempts not to smile, but when I playfully waggle my eyebrows at her and floor the gas pedal again, her laughter bursts through.

"God, what would I do without you?" she says, and my heart ceases in my chest.

"Probably be way less horny," I tease then laugh when she punches me in the arm.

"I'm never horny for you." Her cheeks tint red. I have to wonder if sometimes, when I'm sneaking touches, she secretly likes it.

"Whatever you have to say to get yourself through the day." I release my foot off the brake and peel down the driveway and onto the road.

Then we fly through town with the windows rolled down and a breeze blowing in, heading for the party. We stay there for about forty-five minutes then bail because the cops show up. Ella seems mildly disappointed so I silently vow to make sure she has fun tonight. I drive toward the mountains with music playing from the car speakers. Both of us remain quiet, content.

When we reach the foothills, Ella scoots forward in her seat and spreads her arms out to the side, angling her head back and shutting her eyes. "I wish everything could stay like this forever, just you and me in this car. No parents. No big, scary world. No responsibilities."

"Things can stay this way." I glance back and forth between her and the road, mesmerized by the arch of her chest, her relaxed body, her parted lips. "As long as we're together, we can always have this, no matter where we are."

Usually, she'd agree with me but, like the last couple of weeks, she stays silent.

"Ella, are you sure you're okay?" I ask, gripping the steering wheel. "You've seemed kind of—I don't know— different lately."

She nods but doesn't say anything. I'd press for more, but I don't want to sidetrack her from the few moments of freedom she has, so I bite down on my tongue and bottle up my emotions, telling myself everything will be okay.

We have a plan to stay together forever, and as long as we stick to that plan, everything will be fine.

The Prelude of Ella and Micha

Chapter 5

Ella

I'm having way too much fun. I'm having way too much fun, and I feel guilty. I'm having way too much fun, and I feel guilty about it because I bailed out and left my mother home unsupervised. And the air smells like it's going to rain. It might not seem like much, but every time I have fun and it rains, disaster happens. Like in eleventh grade when I broke my arm snowboarding off the roof. I was having fun and rain was pouring down from the clouds, melting the snow into sleet, making it slippery and causing me to wipe out epically during the landing. Or like when I wrecked my dad's car racing. Then there was the time Micha and I snuck into the local swimming pool and got caught. All rain, rain, rain.

I just hope tonight isn't a repeat of history.

I probably wouldn't be having that much fun, but Micha is ... well, Micha. He knows how to get under my skin and work his way into my psyche. When I was about eight, I seriously thought he could read my mind. Sometimes, I still do.

When we finally pull up to The Hitch—a neglected restaurant that's tucked away near a back road in the middle of the mountains—I know right away that the fun I was having is going to go up to a whole other level, making my guilt soar.

Because we're racing tonight.

And racing equals adrenaline rush.

And adrenaline rush equals tons of fun in drunken Ella land.

Micha slams on the brakes as we near the other cars parked around the flat, dirt area, skidding to a stop right before we run over a crowd of people. A cloud of dust coughs up around the car as Micha shifts into park.

"Are you feeling better?" he asks as he turns the keys and silences the engine.

The hour drive up here has effectively cleared my head of the clutter usually occupying it. "Yep. Much better."

"Good, then I've done my job." He unbuckles his seatbelt then turns to get out of the car. But then he pauses and twists back to face me. "I'm really glad you came with me," he says before he leans over the console to brush his lips across my cheek.

Sober Ella would ream his ass for the move, but drunk Ella kind of likes it. He must not realize I'm that drunk, either, because he quickly hops out of the car before I have a chance to scold him. I hurry after him, reaching for the small bottle of Vodka I stashed in the pocket of my leather jacket as we stride across the gravel and past the parked cars.

Micha eyeballs me as I throw my head back to take a swig. "Where'd you get that?"

"From my house." I screw the cap back on.

He frowns. "How much are you planning on drinking tonight?"

I shrug, maneuvering around so I'm walking backwards in front of him. "As much as it takes to keep the fun going." I do a funky little dance move, and he snorts a laugh.

"Fine." He moves up beside me and drapes an arm around me, navigating me toward a gathered crowd. "But, if I win the race, I'm so joining you."

"Then who will be DD?"

"Guess we'll be spending the night in my car again."

"You know what? That doesn't bother me."

He grins, still staring around as we approach the crowd, the headlights of running cars beaming across the darkness around us. I breathe in the comforting scent of him—cologne mixed with mint and something else that only belongs to Micha.

The rustle of voices and excitement in the air instantly pumps up my adrenaline. I must be shaking with excitement or something because Micha whispers in my ear, "Relax, baby. We'll get to the good part soon."

I roll my eyes yet can't brush off the wild, uncontrollable, fluttering feeling inside my body. I try to keep the sensation contained as we near the group, but it becomes too much, and I finally give up and allow myself to get all bouncy.

Micha laughs at me as I dance to the music playing out of one of the speakers. "And there's my feisty girl. I was worried she wasn't going to come out tonight."

When I let out a playful growl while nipping at him, he chokes on a laugh, nearly buckling over.

"Okay, hand over the bottle," he says, sticking out his hand, still chuckling.

I jut out my lip. "How come?"

"Because you just tried to bite me."

"So? I heard you like to get bit."

He skids to a halt in the dirt. "Where did you hear that from?"

I nonchalantly shrug as I stop in front of him. "There's a rumor going around town that you let Ditzy bite you while you two were messing around."

His jaw drops. "That's so not fucking true."

"So you're saying you don't like it?" I'm totally entertained by his uneasiness since he never gets unsettled. Usually, he's the un-settler.

"No …" He squirms. "I'm not saying that … but I am saying that you're super drunk right now."

"Yeah, maybe I am." I try to see clearly through my drunken mind, but it's a lost cause, and I quickly give up. "So you have been bit by a girl, then?"

He crosses his arms, appearing tense. "Yeah, by you."

My lips part in shock. "When did that happen?"

"We were fifteen and wrestling." He cups his neck. "You bit me right here so I'd let you go. You're such a dirty, little cheat."

I wave him off. "That wasn't a bite. That was a mere teeth nick."

He stares at me unfathomably as his hand falls to his side. "How the hell did we end up in this conversation?"

"Because I'm drunk, and it's funny watching you get all squirmy." Then, just because I can, I spring forward, dip my head, and gently bite his neck. "Ha, ha." I move back, smiling proudly. "Now I stole your first real neck bite."

His jaw is practically hanging to the ground. "I can't believe you just did that."

I bat my eyelashes. "I'm sorry, did you not want to play?"

"No … that's not it." He glances from left to right. When I follow his gaze, I get blindsided by him as he jumps at me. His arms circle my waist, and before I can react, his teeth graze the skin of my throat. "What was that

107

thing you were saying earlier?" He bites at the side of my neck again, and something inside my body explodes. "Payback's a bitch." He pulls away, grinning.

And I stand there, breathless and stunned as I cup my neck.

"Don't start something you can't finish, Ella May." He raises the bottle of vodka he must have stolen from my pocket while he was biting me. "And you can have this back after I win the race." Then he stuffs the bottle into the back pocket of his jeans and starts for the crowd again, doing his swagger walk.

I chase after him, pouting over the bottle and confused over my tingling body.

"What the fuck took you so long?" Ethan Gregory suddenly shoves his way out of the crowd. He is tall and slightly sturdier than Micha with dark hair and lots of tattoos on his arms, and he adds to that growing collection monthly. "You left the shop like three hours ago."

"I had stuff to take care of," Micha replies evasively. He knows that, if he says it has to do with me, Ethan will give me shit. "Besides, I'm here now, so quit getting your panties in a bunch."

"I'm not." Ethan crosses his arms and targets a glare at me. "I just know why you're late because it's always the same reason."

"Fuck you, Gregory," I say, marching toward him.

Micha grabs my hand and pulls me back. "Easy, feisty girl. No fights until after the race."

"Shut the fuck up, Ella," Ethan retorts, and Micha scowls at him.

"You're an ass," I snap at Ethan.

"And you're a bitch," Ethan bites back.

I step forward again with my fists balled at my side, but Micha draws me back by the shoulders

"Okay, you two"—he raises his voice over the bustle of the crowd—"chill the fuck out. I need to focus on racing, not on keeping you two away from each other."

Ethan and I shoot one last death glare at each other but keep our traps shut. Neither of us wants to distract Micha. Drag racing is intense, and if he's frazzled or not in the right place, he could end up crashing into a tree or flipping the car over.

"Thank you," Micha says to both of us before he steers me toward the front of the crowd with his chest pressed against my back.

While I push people out of my way, making a path for us, a few girls scowl at me, but then they notice I'm with Micha and bat their eyelashes at him. When we passed Ditzy, her eyes light up.

"Hey, Micha." She shoots me a dirty look then waves her hand in the air, pressing her boobs against everyone as she makes her way up to us.

I roll my eyes at her and look up at Micha, who dazzles me with a charming grin.

"What?" he says innocently. "Is something bothering you, pretty girl?"

"No." I know I should stop there, or I'm going to end up sounding jealous, but like usual, my mouth takes on a life of its own. "It's just that I don't get it. How can you sleep with someone like her?" I point over my shoulder at Ditzy, who's gotten distracted by a guy with a ponytail.

"Who said I slept with her?" he questions, tapping his chin like he's actually forgotten.

I slap his arm, and he laughs. "You did, last weekend at your party."

He shakes his head, causing strands of his blond hair to fall into his eyes. The moonlight and the headlights highlight his aqua eyes, making them look hauntingly beautiful. If I could have a day where I could draw whatever the hell I wanted to, I would spend hours drawing his eyes.

"I never said I slept with her. You just implied it the next morning when I snuck into your room, and you told me you didn't want me in your bed when I still smelled like skank."

I frown as I remember. "But you never denied that you did."

He shrugs. "I never said it was true, either."

Don't ask it. "Is it true?" *Damn mouth.*

The corners of his mouth threaten to turn upward. "What would you do if I said yes?"

"Nothing." Deep down, though, I know it would annoy the hell out of me, even when I'm drunk. Maybe even more so in my intoxicated state.

He hesitates, his eyes fastened on me, and the intensity

dripping from him is unnerving. "Well, I didn't. In fact, I didn't even kiss her."

I eyeball him over, trying to tell if he's lying. He rarely lies to me, though, and never about the girls he hooks up with. The fact that he hasn't slept with Ditzy makes me stupidly feel better.

"You flirted with her, though," I point out, though it's a moot point. Flirting doesn't matter to Micha. He flirts with everyone, even the sixty-year-old check out lady at the grocery store who smells like cat food.

"So what?" He crooks an eyebrow at me. "I've already told you time and time again that I'm just passing time until you finally come around. Sometimes, I get bored and need to flirt."

I fight back a smile. I shouldn't be glad about this.

Stop it. STOP.

My smile's breaking through.

"Don't smile, pretty girl," he teases as we reach the front of the crowd. "It'll ruin your *I don't give a shit* facade."

"Hey, you promised not to call me that tonight," I remind him in a lame attempt to sidetrack the conversation.

"I'm not forgetting your jealousy that easy," he retorts, his lips tugging into a sexy half-grin.

I chew on my thumbnail as I take in the cars parked around us, refusing to focus on him. There's Danny's 1971 Dodge Challenger, Mikey's 1968 Camaro, and Benny's 1970 GTO, which I'm secretly in love with, though I'll never admit it to Micha, because it'll hurt his feelings.

"So, tell me this." Micha steps up beside me and sketches circles on my upper arm as he stares at the line of cars across from us. "Why does the idea of me sleeping with her bother you so much?"

"Because she's not good enough for you," I say truthfully with a shrug. Then I casually reach over and steal the bottle of vodka from his pocket.

He gives me a suspicious sidelong glance. "Who *is* good enough for me? You?" He's joking, but it triggers a hidden nerve. I think about how I'm about to bail on him and our plans in a month, just leave him in this dump of a town.

It feels like invisible fingers have wrapped around my

113

throat. "No, Micha, not me." I slip out from under his arm. "I'm in no way good enough for you." I back through the crowd, my heart throbbing in my chest. "I'll be right back." I reel around and run back to the car.

After I hop into the backseat, I unscrew the cap from the bottle and take a few sips before resting back. One day, and hopefully soon, Micha is going to realize just how amazing he is and start looking for girls who have substance instead of girls like Ditzy. Then these little moments in this town—with me and everyone else—will just be moments that he'll eventually forget about.

I'll become a fading memory along with everything I did. Even when I break my promise to him.

Chapter 6

Micha

I said the wrong damn thing. I knew I did as soon as I said it, but I get so sick of her thinking that I'm still sleeping around with everyone, because I'm not. I can't anymore, not when I feel the way I do about her.

I can't think of a way to recover from my mess up, and she ends up running off somewhere. I don't chase her down since she'll keep running from me if I do. If I give her a few minutes to clear her head, she'll more than likely come back and pretend nothing happened.

I remain focused on the race, feeling a little better when I get challenged by Stanford and his Mustang because it's gotta fucking weak sauce engine.

I'm about to go back to my car, ready to roll, but Ella still hasn't come back to me. My head is a little foggy as I scan the crowd for her and then by the rundown restaurant where a few people are getting high. Ella's not usually into that, but she can also get really random and end up doing a lot of stupid shit sometimes. Still, she's not back there. And, as I'm heading back to the crowd, Ethan finds me.

"Just get in the damn car," he says, giving me a shove in the back. He doesn't race, but he's obsessed with me winning. He puts a lot of work into my car and engine; therefore, 'we share the win.' "I'll drive with you if you can't find her."

Frowning, I hike across the dirt toward my car, swinging the keys around my finger. "Just look for her, okay? And don't say anything stupid when you find her and piss her off."

"You know that's not possible." He backs toward the lineup area where two cars are parked side by side. "If I say anything to her, she's going to get pissed at me. The only person she never does that with is you."

He's right. The two of them clash more than my parents did before my dad bailed.

Running out of time, I spin on my heels and jog back to my car, trying to tell myself that it'll be okay.

I can race without her in the car. I don't have to worry

about her.

When I reach my car, though, I suddenly feel better.

Ella's lying on the backseat, staring up at the stars through the rolled down window with the bottle of Vodka in her hand.

I rest my arms on windowsill. "Did you finish the bottle off?"

She shakes her head without looking at me. "No." She raises the bottle so I can see the liquid splashing inside it. "I took a few shots, though."

A breath eases from my lips as I open the door. "Do you want me to take you home so we can talk?"

Her eyes cut in my direction. "What? No. Why?"

My shoulders unravel as I hop into the seat and shut the door. "You just seem upset, and I have a feeling I might be making the night worse."

She eyes me for an eternity then finally sits up, screws the lid back on the bottle, and drops it onto the floor. She scoots forward in the seat and rests her elbows on the console. "I'm fine." She tugs the elastic out of her hair and shakes it out. "Sorry for flipping out. I'm going to be chill for the rest of the night. I swear. And I totally get if you don't want me to ride with you now. I'm being distracting."

"You're perfectly fine ..." I bite on my bottom lip as I watch her comb her fingers through her hair. My hands start to ache when she angles her head back, her chest arching forward as her eyelids slip shut. I could write a thousand songs just about the way she looks right now, and a thousand more about the way she makes me feel.

When she lifts her head up again, her eyes open, and she encounters my hungry gaze.

I quickly clear my throat and look away before I end up doing something stupid. "You know I always want you to ride with me, even when you're upset. And when you're being distracting."

She remains silent for a while, and when she does speak again, her voice is soft, almost breathless. "Micha?"

I grip the steering wheel, staring at the trees enclosing the area, praying she'll finally reveal that she loves me, too.

But all she says is, "Nothing. Never mind. I'll tell you later."

I can barely breathe, let alone press her. "Okay, sounds

good." I shift the car into drive. "Are you ready for this?"

Nodding, she drunkenly dives over the console, eliciting a laugh from me. She pushes up and gets situated before waving me forward. "Let's get this show on the road."

"Seat belt first," I say. When she frowns, I add, "Your safety always comes first, beautiful."

She sighs then pulls the strap over her chest. "Fine, but the same goes for you."

I do as she asks, buckling myself in. "Thanks. Glad my safety does come first and that you think I'm beautiful."

She shakes her head yet doesn't disagree.

I drive up to the starting line, feeling a bit calmer. But, my nerves start to get rattled as I wait for Stanford's girlfriend to flag us off. I thrum my fingers on my knees, fiddling with the stereo, doing just about everything to chill the fuck out.

"Would you relax?" Ella says, placing a hand on my bouncing knee. "You'll do well. You always do."

My gaze slides from her hand on my leg to her eyes. "I know, but I always get so fucking fidgety right before flag off. I get stuck in my own head."

"I know you do." She ponders something then her green eyes light up. "I have an idea." She reaches forward and picks up my iPod from the dock on the cracked dash. Scrolling through the songs, she selects, "The Distance" by Cake, and cranks it up full blast until the speakers crackle and the windshield vibrates.

"Now you can't hear your own thoughts!" she shouts over the music, laughing.

I laugh with her. "Thank you!"

Her gorgeous lips expand to a grin. "Anytime." Then she places her hand on my knee as if it belongs there.

And, in my opinion, it does.

I bob my head as I wait for the flag to get dropped. Ella's fingers tighten on my knee as Stanford's girlfriend strolls up between the cars.

"On your mark," she starts with the flag raised. "Get set. Go!"

We peel out of the parking lot and fly down the road toward the trees, side by side with the Mustang. There's something unstably beautiful about racing, liberating even.

But, what's really beautiful about the scene is how much Ella gets turned on by the dangerous thrill of it. Put the girl in a car pressing a hundred miles an hour, and she damn near orgasms. It's hard to pay attention as she lets go of my knee and sticks her arm out the window, as if she's catching the air. Her other hand wanders to her stomach, her fingers grazing across the bottom of her shirt, like she's considering touching herself.

Yes, please touch yourself. Good God, touching you—

"Micha, look out!" she shouts, her eyes widening as her arm shoots out for the dashboard.

My attention whips to the road, which we're reaching the end of. I brake hard and crane the wheel. The car spins wildly, the tires screeching and kicking up dirt. I manage to get it under control and head back toward the finish line, though.

"Holy shit," Ella breathes as the song ends. Then she busts up laughing, drunk and reckless and free. "That was intense."

I laugh with her, but I'm a bit distraught. The cruel, harsh reality of what just happened weighs heavily inside me. I damn near killed us, all because I couldn't keep my dirty thoughts under control.

This is getting out of hand.

Maybe it's time to tell her, just spell out how I feel. Because, if I don't, I damn near might end up killing the both of us.

Chapter 7

Ella

"It's celebration time!" I exclaim as I hop out of the Chevelle with the bottle of Vodka lifted in the air.

Micha's long legs stretch as he climbs out the car. "Celebrate away." He doesn't seem as happy as he should be, which makes me sad.

"What's wrong?" I ask as I round the car toward him.

"Nothing's wrong." He watches me while I unscrew the lid off the vodka, slant my head back, and take a long gulp.

"You look awfully upset for someone who just kicked some ass." I wipe the burning liquid from my lips with the back of my hand and stare out at the bonfire someone started. "Is it because you almost wrecked at the end of the road? It happens to the best of us."

He studies me intently before snatching the bottle from my hand and downing a shot himself. "You and I need to

123

talk later about something," he says nervously as he removes the mouth of the bottle from his lips. "But, first, let's celebrate."

I pause, wondering what the hell he wants to talk about, worried he might know what I want to talk to him about. That's when the rush of alcohol hits me square in the brain, and all I want to do is have fun, not think.

I grab the bottle from him, throw back another swallow, and then skip drunkenly toward the fire. He calls after me, laughing, but I continue to prance until I spot Renee, dancing on the tailgate of Ethan's truck. It looks fun, so I jump up with her. She claps her hands together excitedly.

"Yeah! Drunk Ella is out tonight!" she shouts as she pumps a hand up in the air and wiggles her hips.

"Hell yeah, she is!" As I jiggle my ass to the music, the glow of the headlights and fire surrounding me, and the worries of the day dwindle away.

What a perfect night, I think. *And I thought it was going to be shitty.*

Then, moments later, I smell the rain.

The fucking rain, like an omen.

No, I'm not going to let it ruin my night.

I throw back another shot. Then another. Until my mind is spinning and any thoughts of this night getting ruined fade away. I start to dance. And, I mean, really dance. The kind of dancing people only do behind closed doors, yet I'm out in the open, right in the spotlight, and I don't give a shit.

"Hey, I thought we were supposed to be sharing." Micha suddenly appears beside the tailgate. His chin is tipped up and he's staring at me as I rock out.

"What? You want this?" I wiggle the bottle in his direction. When he extends his fingers for it, I whip my hand back out of his reach.

"Oh, so you want to play dirty tonight, huh?" he teases with a playful smile.

I smirk at him then throw back my head and suck down a swallow.

His smile darkens, and without warning, he reaches up and snags me by the hips. A gasp escapes my lips as he jerks me forward and lifts me up and off the tailgate.

"No fair!" I cry through my laughter as he sets me

down on the tailgate with my legs dangling over the edge.

"How is that not fair?" he asks, spreading my legs open and positioning himself between them.

I shrug. There was no real logic behind my statement. "I have no idea."

"You're so drunk." He shakes his head as he reaches for the bottle in my hand.

Again, I move it away from him, tucking my hand behind my back. He decides to play dirty and starts tickling my side. I let out a screech while I fall back into the bed of the truck, nearly landing on Renee's feet. She skitters out of the way as Micha clambers up into the bed, chasing after me, his body gliding up mine until we're hip to hip, chest to chest, face to face. Lip to lip.

It feels like I should be fleeing from his nearness, but I'm too stupidly content at the moment to put up a fuss.

"This feels nice," I say with a content sigh, relaxing under Micha's body.

A pucker forms at his brow. "I think I might need to cut you off ..." He trails off as I loop my arms around his neck.

"No way. I'm having too much fun."

His breath catches in his throat as I graze my fingers up and down the nape of his neck. His reaction makes me giggle for some reason.

"God, I love it when you're like this," he whispers, lowering his forehead to mine. "I just wish you weren't so drunk."

"Me too," I agree, but I'm not quite sure what I'm agreeing to.

As his hot breath dusts my cheeks, I have the strongest urge to touch his lips.

So I do.

Moving my fingers around to his face, I graze the pad of my thumb across his lip ring, drawing a soft line over his bottom lip.

His breath hitches. "Ella ..." It almost sounds like he groans, but that's probably the drunken side of my mind hearing things. My alcohol level is also more than likely the cause behind why it feels like he kisses my thumb and gently bites on it. Or maybe that's just payback for the bite and lick I did to him earlier.

Whatever. I don't really care right now.

"Can we go play?" I lean back and bat my eyelashes at him. "Pretty please."

His low chuckle reverberates through my body. "We can do whatever you want." With a deep sigh, he pushes back. Then he steals the bottle from my hand before bounding off the tailgate.

"Cheater!" I cry, flipping Renee the bird when she gives me *the look*. It's the same one she's been giving me for the entire summer every time Micha and I act like this, which yes, is a lot. But that's what we do. Have fun. As friends. It makes me realize how much I truly need him, how much I don't want to be a fading memory for him.

Maybe this running off to Vegas thing will be harder than I thought.

Maybe I could just ask him to come with me.

Could I do that?

Is it really that easy?

With Micha, everything is easy.

I run to the edge of the tailgate and jump onto Micha's back mid-swig. He grunts from the contact as I fasten my arms and legs around him. "Don't finish that off!" I try to reach for the bottle, but he spins around as he continues to drink. "Micha Scott! You are the biggest cheater ever!"

Once he's done with his drink, he screws the lid back on and then tosses the bottle to Ethan, who's shaking his head at us.

"You two are fucking crazy," Ethan remarks, opening the bottle.

"Ethan Gregory, don't you dare finish that off!" I cry, but my plea fades as Micha holds onto my legs and hikes toward the fire with me on his back.

"Are you going to carry me around like this all night?" I ask as he approaches Stanford, Benny, and Grantford along with a group of girls I used to go to school with.

"Maybe." He grips onto me tighter. "At least as long as you'll let me."

"That might be a very long time because the stars are spinning a lot tonight." I glance up at the sky and cringe at the thick clouds. I summon a deep breath. Even through the fogginess in my body, I can still smell it.

Impending rain.

An impending warning.

Chapter 8

Micha

There is no way in hell I'm going to put her down, not after what just happened. I don't care if she's drunk. Fuck, I'm feeling pretty drunk myself. With Ella on my back, I feel both high and drunk.

She fucking touched my lips. Let me kiss her thumb. Let me press my body against hers.

And now she's on my back.

"Hey, Micha." Benny gives me the chin nod as I approach some other racers with Ella on my back. She's been on there for about five minutes and hasn't shown any signs of wanting to get down.

"Hey, man." I nod back, noting the strange look he gives me and Ella. The look is fleeting and quickly vanishes, as if he's been expecting this sort of thing to happen. I saw Ethan and Renee give me the same look, and I'm fucking hoping maybe they're right.

131

Something's changed. I can feel it in the air.

Right as I think that, thunder rumbles from the sky. It's followed by the drizzle of rain. Everyone starts to scatter for their cars as the raindrops put out the fire and drench everyone's clothes. Ella holds onto me tightly as I sprint for the car, slipping in the mud and struggling to see straight. I manage to get her in the passenger side safely then get my own ass into the driver's seat where I turn the engine on and crank up the heat.

"We're so screwed," she remarks, staring at the raindrops splattering across the window.

Her damp, auburn hair rests on her shoulders, beads of water trickling down her cheeks and lips. As she slips off her jacket, I relish in the sight of her tank top clinging to her body. I can't help thinking about how I saw her nipples through that shirt this afternoon and how turned on I was.

"Micha, did you hear me?" she asks, wiping some raindrops from her forehead with the back of her hand.

I shake my head, too drunk to be ashamed of the direction of my gaze. "Not a damn word."

She laughs, but it's off pitch. "I asked what we're going to do. Neither of us are sober enough to drive. And I'm guessing from all the cars still parked that everyone else might be in the same condition."

I shrug, blinking my focus back to her face. "I guess we'll have to just chill here until we sober up. I'm not super drunk, so I'll probably only need an hour or so."

She presses her lips together, her gaze relentless until she finally clumsily hops over the console and falls into the backseat. "Well, I'm getting comfortable, then. There's a good chance I'll end up passing out."

"Not fair." I rotate in the seat and watch her stretch her legs out. "How come I have to stay up here?"

"Who said you have to stay up there?" she questions, wringing out her hair.

Taking that as an open invitation, I turn on some music then tumble over the console, probably a little too eagerly, and end up bumping my elbow into her stomach.

"Micha," she grunts and then laughs as I force her to lean forward and then climb on the seat behind her. "That was probably the most unsmooth I've ever seen you act."

"Yeah, maybe." I position us so both our legs are

stretched out across the seat and my back is against the door. Then I guide her toward me until her back is resting against my chest. "This is nice," I admit.

"We've sat like this before." She jumps as thunder booms and lightning snaps just outside. "Probably too much … people are starting to think stuff."

"Oh, yeah?" I comb my fingers through her wet hair. "Like what?"

She shrugs then reclines back and rests her head against my chest. Her ear is very close to my heart, and I worry she'll hear how rapidly it's beating. *What will she think if she hears it? Does it matter? You were going to tell her anyway. Tell her!*

"They think we're a couple," she says before I can get a chance to pour my heart out. "Which is a little weird considering you fool around with other people all the time. I mean, what do they think? We have, like, an open relationship or something?"

"I already told you I've been chilling on getting laid," I tell her. When her back goes rigid, I quickly move my hands to her shoulders and gently press my fingertips into her skin, massaging her tense muscles. "Maybe that's why they think it. Perhaps they think my celibacy is because I'm with you."

"Well, that's still insulting." Her head falls to the side as I continue to shower her muscles with attention.

"And why's that?"

"Because ... it means they think we are having..."

"Sex." I smash my lips together, trying not to laugh at her slight embarrassment over the subject. The girl can rock out solo in front of a ton of people, but talk about anything sexual, and she grows uneasy.

"Are you laughing at me?" She starts to turn her head, but I move my fingers downward, splaying them across her collarbone, and she sinks into the touch.

"No way." I rest my forehead on the back of her head. Her hair smells like rain, and I inhale the delicious scent, branding it into my mind, branding this moment into my mind forever. "You smell so good."

"This feels so good." She moans, the kind of moan I imagine would leave her lips if I was thrusting inside her.

A low moan escapes my own lips as I battle to remain

in control over myself. But I can feel my willpower fraying, about to break.

"Ella, there's something I need to tell you." I kiss the back of her head, making a path downward.

"Yeah, me, too ... it's about our pact." She sighs into me. "Maybe we could go somewhere else."

"Like where?" I nuzzle my face into her neck. "I've always thought California was an awesome place. I mean, I know it's a little bit more expensive, and we'll need to probably stick around here a little bit longer to save up, but I like our plan."

"But what if I told you there was somewhere else I really wanted to go? And soon."

"Then I'd listen. You know I'll always listen to you. So what's up? What plan are you conjuring up in that beautiful head of yours?"

"Well, I got acc—" Her phone vibrates from inside her pocket and cuts her off.

Sighing, she fishes it out then mumbles, "Who the hell is that?" She puts the phone up to her ear. "Hello?" she answers tentatively.

"Ella, where are you?" Her dad's loud voice can be heard clearly through the cab of the car.

"Um, out and about." She glances at the clouds in the sky. "Where are you?"

"You need to get home," he slurs. "You have mom duty. God dammit, Ella, I already told you this. What the fuck is wrong with you?"

"But I ..." She touches her numb lips then looks over her shoulder at me. "It might take a while."

"About an hour," I whisper, hugging her against me.

"About an hour," she tells her dad.

"Whatever," her dad snaps. "Just get your ass home." With that, he hangs up, and I grit my teeth, pissed that he ruined her night.

"I should have stayed home," she yawns tiredly, switching her phone to the text screen.

"What are you doing?" I brush her hair from her shoulder and peer over to read what she's typing.

"Texting my mom." Her fingers move across the buttons. "Making sure everything's okay. Hopefully she'll respond."

137

Ella: Mom, r u ok?

It takes a minute before she responds.

Mom: I'm fine.

Ella: Is this mom?

Mom: Of course, baby girl.

The endearing name makes Ella relax.

Ella: I'll be home soon. Just stay in your room, okay?

Mom: Of course, baby girl. C you soon.

"I need to sober up," Ella mutters as she stuffs her phone into her pocket.

"I'll get you home as soon as I can, okay?" I promise her. "You just try to relax."

"That's the problem. I'm too relaxed. I never should have gone out tonight."

"You're fine," I whisper, stroking her cheek with my fingers.

She sinks deeply into my touch with a sigh. A few minutes later, her breathing softens as she passes out.

An hour later, I'm sober enough to drive home, and I buckle Ella into the backseat and head down the muddy road toward town. By the time I pull up into her driveway, Ella's awake yet still completely out of it.

"Wow, that was a short drive home," she mutters, rubbing her bloodshot eyes then slipping her jacket on.

"It took as long as it always takes." I hop out of the car, my boots splashing in the puddles, and help her get out of the backseat.

"It still felt really short." She stretches her arms above her head and yawns. "Hey, it stopped raining. I'm so glad."

"And why's that?"

"Because the rain is bad."

I'd ask her to elaborate more, but she's pretty incoherent. In fact, I wouldn't be surprised if she can't remember what happened in the car come morning.

She can barely walk, so I help her climb up her tree; otherwise, she'd probably fall and break her neck. But I don't mind. I actually enjoy it. Helping Ella is my thing, and I want it to be my thing for a very long time.

I need to tell her.

As I'm getting ready to climb back down the tree, she beckons me back to her and throws her arms around my neck. "You're my hero. You know that?" She kisses my cheek.

I can't help it. When she turns her head, I kiss her right on her lips. The kiss is soft, innocent, but by the time I pull away, I've decided. Tomorrow, I'm going to tell her how I feel.

Chapter 9

Ella

The night seemed like it was going to turn out okay, even with the rainstorm and my dad ruining it toward the end. Micha gave me a massage. Things got a bit intense, though in a good way, I think. I almost told him about Vegas, almost asked him to come with me. But the vodka got to me, and I fell asleep.

As my eyelids drifted shut, I silently vowed I'd tell Micha tomorrow when I was sober because I'm starting to realize how much I need him.

Then I got home and everything changed in a heartbeat.

I thought, since the rain had stopped, the night would remain all right, that the storm had passed and skipped over me this time.

But the storm was just waiting for me on the inside of my house.

My mother is dead.

My mother took her own life.

And the house is so quiet.

Because my father is gone.

He told me to come home.

Told me I was on mom duty.

Told me.

Told me.

Told me.

Yet I didn't come back for over an hour.

As I stand in the doorway, staring at the bathroom floor that's painted red with blood, the soundlessness of the house encompasses me.

Maybe I should make some noise. Break the silence. Break myself.

I think I screamed. Maybe. I'm not sure.

I finally cross the room and check her pulse, but the bathtub water is as thick as red paint, so I already know.

She's dead.

And her skin is unbelievably cold.

Like the chill of the rain.

I blow out the most deafening breath as I walk back to the doorway and call the police with my phone. Then I wait. For what, I'm not sure. Maybe the rain to start up again.

Keep an eye on your mother.

She's gone.

Keep an eye on your mother.

I knew I should have stayed home.

Keep an eye on your mother.

This is all your fault.

Somehow, within the next few minutes, Micha shows up and holds me. I don't even know how he knows, but he does. He tells me it's going to be okay, tells me he'll take care of me.

"No," is the only reply I can get out.

"This isn't your fault," he whispers, hugging me tightly. It's like he knows what's going on inside my head, always does.

"Yes, it is," I say numbly. "It really, really is."

This is all your fault.

"I don't deserve to be held, Micha."

He doesn't let me go, even when the paramedics show up and take her out of the water. They seal her up in a body bag and wheel her lifeless body out toward the flashing red and blue lights. Then we follow them to the front lawn where I see my dad. He's standing there, staring at the ambulance, crying, crying, sobbing.

This is all your fault.

I push away from Micha and stumble to my dad. I need to tell him I'm sorry for leaving, for not coming home, for not doing better. For being selfish. But when he looks at me, I already know that no amount of sorrys is ever going to cut it.

"This is all your fault," he says, sounding more sober than he ever has before.

"I'm sorry," I whisper, my voice getting lost in the wind.

"Just get in the car," he snaps with tears in his eyes. "We need to go to the hospital."

Nodding, I follow him up the driveway with my head hung low, ignoring Micha when he calls out to me.

I can't look at him.

Right now.

Never again.

Look anyone in the eye.

After what I did.

I slide into the driver's seat, my dad not well enough to drive. Then I follow the ambulance through the neighborhood and toward the bridge that exits the town and leads to the closet hospital.

As we cross over the darkened water, I remember the last time I was here. With my mother.

She said she could fly.

She believed that she was invincible.

But she wasn't.

All because of me.

Chapter 10

2 weeks later...

Ella

I wish I could go back to the sprinkler days, those afternoons when Micha and I would run around his front yard, getting wet. Life was so simple back then, so promising. Nothing is promising anymore.

The funeral is unbearable, yet I manage to get through it, even when my brother Dean informs me that he blames me also. After that, I spend most of my days cleaning the house. It's the only thing I can focus on that doesn't make my brain feel like it's going to explode from the guilt. The only time I can fully breathe is when my father is gone; otherwise, he's at the house and looking at me like I ruined everything.

Because I did.

As I pack up the clutter in my mother's bedroom, I feel the truth weighing heavily inside me, like I did when they closed the lid of her coffin. Her death is my burden to carry. Forever.

With each of her belongings I put into the box, the weight grows heavier while repetitive questions replay in my head over and over again.

Is that what she wanted when she did it? To get rid of the burden? To leave this all behind? Her belongings? What was she thinking? Could I have stopped her if I was here? I did once before. That day she went down to the bridge. But I wasn't here this time.

I'm pretty sure I can fly, Ella May. The last words she ever spoke to me flow through my head. She had to be in the same mindset. Why didn't I see it? Why am I such a bad daughter?

Why?

Why?

Why?

"Why did you think you could fly, Mom?" I whisper as I clutch onto a necklace that once belonged to her. "What went on in that head of yours?"

Setting the necklace down, I place the box on the unmade bed and open the nightstand drawer to take out the pills she once almost overdosed on. She took a few before she slit her wrists the final night she was alive—at least that's what the medical examiner said.

Not truly understanding why I do it, I pop two of her pills into my mouth and swallow them, feeling the strangest bit closer to her the moment they slip down my throat and settle into my body.

As the pills seep through my bloodstream, I wander down to the kitchen to do the dishes, feeling slightly dizzy. The way the water moves is odd. The air smells weird, too, like grease and smoke.

Is this how she saw the world?

"I'm headed out," my dad slurs as he staggers into the kitchen.

Elbow deep in pan grease, all I do is nod.

"I might not be home tonight, just so you know."

I peer over my shoulder at him. "Okay."

He lingers by the back door while he clumsily slips his jacket on. He hasn't been sober since the night my mom died, and he has been binge drinking every night at the bar since the funeral.

"Be safe," I feel the need to say.

He blinks at me like I've slapped him. "God, you look so much like her," he mutters as he reaches for the back door. "It hurts to even look at you anymore." Then he storms out, slamming the door behind him.

It seems like I should cry, but I think my tear ducts broke the night I found her.

Everything broke.

After I finish up the dishes, I trudge up to my room with my father's words echoing in my mind.

It hurts to even look at you anymore.

Hurts.

Everything hurts.

I stand in front of the mirror on my wall, wondering if maybe he's right. I do look so much like her. Leaning forward, I squint at my own eyes that are squinting back at me. For the briefest moment, something painful flashes across my expression.

The truth.

Of who I am.

My reflection can see it.

What I did.

Panicking, I rip the sheet from the bed and throw it over the mirror, breathing heavily. Is this what everyone sees when they look at me? What I did? What I caused?

"I need to get out of here." I hurry out of my bedroom, bolt down the stairs, and then outside. I start to jog down the driveway—run, run, run away—when I hear Micha call out my name.

"What are you doing?" he asks over the sound of his boots thudding against the concrete as he jogs after me.

I almost keep going, keep running to the end of the driveway. When I get there, I'll turn right and go to the bus stop. Then I'll buy a one-way ticket out of here. Leave everything behind, including myself.

"Baby, did you hear me?" The sadness in his voice stings at my heart and my guilt.

I want to scream at him not to call me baby. I don't deserve such an endearing name, don't deserve him. Yet he seems to think the opposite, refusing to leave my side unless I lock myself in the house. Micha knows I'm breaking, and he wants to stop it, but I don't deserve to stop breaking.

I halt and stare down the driveway at the neighbor's kids across the street who are running through the sprinklers. Happy. He should be happy. Not sad.

"I don't know."

The fence rattles as he hops over it and then hurries up behind me. "Is everything okay?"

"Yes."

"I ..." When he reaches me, he lowers his face and puts his mouth beside my ear. "What do you need from me? Please, tell me what you need."

I squeeze my eyes shut. His nearness is painful. His nearness reminds me of the night two weeks ago when everything was perfect.

And then it wasn't.

"I just need ..." I open my eyes and dare to look at him. The worry in his aqua gaze makes me instantly regret it, though. Micha sees everything inside me. He has to see the ugliness in me right now.

I should run back into the house and away from him, but I don't want to go back into that house. Into *her* house. Into the quiet. With myself and my stupid all-revealing reflection.

I'm pretty sure I can fly, Ella May.

She thought she could fly.

Why did she think that so much?

I need to understand.

And there might be a way.

"I need to go somewhere," I say to Micha. "To the party going on. By the bridge."

Chapter 11

Micha

For the first time in my life, I can't help Ella. I'm trying the best I can, but she won't open up to me. Maybe that's why I drive her to the party, even though it's clear she's out of it, either drunk or on something. With the largeness of her pupils, my guess is the latter.

The ride up to the party is agonizingly quiet, nowhere near the comfortable silence we used to share. For most of the journey, Ella stares out the window with her arms crossed, watching the mountains, hills, and then the bridge roll by.

"My mom used to think she could fly," Ella mutters suddenly as the car reaches the center of the bridge. "She would say so all the time. She even thought she could fly off that bridge."

I open my mouth to say something, but I have no clue what that something should be. I feel so helpless all the time. I fucking hate it.

"You don't need to say anything." She shuts her eyes and rests her head against the window, curling up within herself. "I was just mumbling nonsense."

My heart is breaking for her. God, I wish it was the only one breaking, wish I could bear her pain. She thinks it's her fault. She told me that. I've told her a thousand times that it's not, yet I can't seem to change her mind. Her stupid, asshole father and brother aren't helping at all, either. Both have put the blame on her.

Fucking bastards.

We make the rest of the drive in silence again. As soon as we arrive at the party, Ella hops out and heads straight for the alcohol. The party is going full force, music blaring, a bonfire blazing in the trees. Half the damn town is here. Mad chaos fills the air, but that's typical. I used to love it, but right now, I'm starting to wonder if I shouldn't have brought Ella here.

"We should go to our spot," I suggest to her an hour into the party, "or somewhere more quiet."

"You can go wherever you want," she replies, sipping

her beer. "You don't need to babysit me."

I frown as I scan the rambunctious crowd, the bonfire, the noise, and then her. Since that night, dark circles have permanently resided beneath those gorgeous eyes of hers. Her skin is pale, and I think she's been losing weight. I want to call her out on her weight loss, but I'm afraid I'll push her to the edge.

"I love babysitting you, though," I attempt to joke like we used to all the time. I drape my arm around her shoulder and pull her closer, refusing to let her out of my sight for the night. "It's my favorite job in the world."

She tenses then ducks out from under my arm. "Well, I don't want you to." She stumbles away toward the fire, gripping the beer bottle in her hand.

I smash my lips together, my body trembling as I begin to curse the stars above us, only it's cloudy and I can't see them. So, instead, I curse the clouds.

Everything seemed absolutely great two weeks ago. I was going to tell Ella how I felt, and it seemed slightly possible that she felt the same way. But everything's reversing now.

Everything's gone.

My beautiful, wild, carefree Ella is gone.

I want to cry. Tears are actually starting to sting at my eyes. Unsure I'll be able to hold them in, I start for my car so I won't break down in front of half the town.

I make it three steps before someone steps in front of me and blocks my path.

"Hey, Micha." Some woman who looks vaguely familiar touches my shoulder. "How's it going?"

I shake my head, annoyed and still on the verge of crying. "Can you move please? I need to get to my car."

She giggles as she strokes my arm. "Want some company?"

"No." My tone is clipped.

She presses her chest against mine. "Give me five minutes," she whispers in my ear. "Bet I can change your mind."

I remember the last couple of years when I let women distract me from Ella, but the idea of doing so right now seems completely fucking wrong. Plus, I doubt it will help. Nothing will help except getting my Ella back.

Without responding, I dodge around her and hurry for my Chevelle parked out in the midst of a ton of other cars. As soon as I sink into the driver's seat, I shut the door and let a few tears fall freely. After a few minutes, I collect myself and climb back out to find Ella, who seems to be nowhere. I grow worried as I head for Ethan's truck where he's chatting with Renee.

"Hey, have either of you seen Ella?" I jerk my hand through my hair as I scan the throng of intoxicated people, searching for her fiery red hair in the midst.

"Yeah, she took off with Grantford somewhere," Renee tells me, resting back on her hands. "She told me something about going to the bridge … I don't know … She seemed pretty out of it."

My heart slams inside my chest as I recollect what Ella said earlier, how her mom thought she could fly off the bridge.

No … She wouldn't … Would she?

I don't think.

I just run to my car and drive like mad toward the bridge.

***

It starts to rain on my way there. Downpour. Lightning flashes. Thunder grumbles. The scene is like two weeks ago when Ella and I stayed in my car. It feels like an eternity has passed since then, the memory fading. It makes me want to cry again, bawl my fucking heart out until I can't breathe. But I can't break down right now, so I drive until I reach the bridge.

The sight knocks the wind out of me. It's worse than I imagined. Ella's out on a beam that extends over the blackened water, the rain streaming down from the clouds. All I can think as I hop out of my car and run toward her is that I'm going to lose her.

I can't *lose her.*

"Ella, what are you doing?" I shout as I stumble to a halt near the railing and grasp the metal beams of the bridge. "Get down from there. You're going to hurt yourself." With little hesitancy, I hoist myself up.

"I don't think I will," she insists with her arms stretched out to the side. "I think I might be able to fly … just like her."

"Your mom couldn't fly." Balancing, I inch my way across the beam toward her while trying not to look down at the deep water—reality—below us. "What are you on?"

"I took one of her old pills." She tips her head back and rain showers across her face. "I wanted to see what it was like for her."

"Your mother didn't know better, but you do." Gripping onto the metal wire above my head, I reach my other hand for her, my fingers trembling with the fear that I won't get to her in time. *Stay calm. Don't panic. Just get her off of here.* "Now come over here. You're scaring the shit out of me."

"I don't know if I can." She gradually rotates around and faces me and my fear escalates. *God, please, please don't let her fall. Please.* "I'm not sure if I want to."

"Yes, you do. You're stronger than that." I move closer to her, reaching for her, needing her. Right now. "Please, just get over here."

Her body leans and starts to drift to the side.

A part of me dies, right there on the bridge, a part of me I'll never get back.

159

"I swear to God, Ella!" I shout. "Give me your hand!"

She abruptly snaps out of her trance then stands up straight and grasps my hand. As our fingers entwine, I pant heavily. I just came so close to losing her, and I've never told her I love her.

I can never lose her.

I need to tell her I love her.

Once I get us both off the beam, I circle my arms around her and clutch onto her with everything I have in me. "I'm never going to let you go. I love you. Please, don't leave me," I whisper so soundlessly the pitter patter of the rain swallows up my voice. Leaning back, I smooth her wet hair out of her face and speak lucidly this time. "Don't you ever do that to me again. I can't do this without you."

"Micha, I ..." She slants her head back and blinks against the drizzle of the rain as she peers up at me. "I'm sorry." She embraces me back, her arms wrapping around my waist. "I didn't want to think anymore. It was just too much, and my mind wouldn't slow down. But it's all right now. I can think clearly again."

"Next time come to me, don't just run. *Please.* I know things are hard right now, but it'll get better. We've always made it through every single bad thing thrown at us." I summon a breath, preparing to say what I needed to two weeks ago, the most important thing I will ever say. "Ella, I love—"

Her lips crash against mine, and moments later, our tongues tangle as our bodies align. She kisses me wholly. *She* kisses *me* for the first time. Right there in the middle of the rain.

I try to tell myself the moment is perfect. That everything will be okay. That it's the most mind-blowing, life-changing kiss I've ever experienced. And it is. But, it's also the most heart-wrenching, soul-breaking kiss I've ever had and will ever endure.

When she pulls away, I can see exactly how not okay everything is with her. With us. Exactly how imperfect the moment is. Because it's only a fragment of my Ella looking up at me, one that doesn't want to be here. With me. Be here at all.

I want to say something perfect that will fix this.

Want to say *anything*.

But there are no perfect words.

I'm not sure if anything will be perfect again.

I won't stop trying, though.

Ever.

Until I bring my Ella back.

Chapter 12

Ella

The morning after Micha talked me down from the bridge, I wake up in my bed with the soft scent of his cologne filling my heart. I'm wearing his T-shirt, and my hair smells like rain.

"What happened?" I mutter as I sit up, running my fingers through my tangled hair. My entire body aches almost as much as my soul. "Something happened last night. Something's different."

Faint memories of a breathtaking kiss surface along with the haunting image of a bridge. Then a much darker, hazier image emerges. *Me in a car. Warmth. Fear.* So much fear that it makes me feel terrified right now. Fogginess fills my head, yet somehow, my vision is crystal clear. I know what I have to do to survive.

I need to leave everything behind.

This house.

My dad.

This town.

Micha.

Shaking thoughts of my best friend from my mind, I drag my ass out of bed and rush to pack some clothes into my duffel bag along with my sketchbook. I leave most of my stuff behind, not wanting to take anything that will remind me of myself on this journey.

I also grab my acceptance letter from underneath my pillow and scrounge the house for what cash I can find, adding it to my own pile. It's not much, but it'll get me a bus ticket to Vegas and a new start.

I don't tell my father good-bye before I leave the house. I don't want to see the hurt in his eyes anymore — hurt him more.

Slinging my bag over my shoulder, I hike down the driveway toward the street. The sun is rising, the sky painting the land an orange pink. It's my final sunrise in this town, my final everything of this life.

As I reach the end of the concrete, I pause to glance back at Micha's house. A small part of me begs to go there, whispers that I'm leaving the love of my life behind.

"I'm sorry for breaking our pact," I whisper as I turn away. "But it's for the best that you stay away from me; otherwise, I'll ruin you, too."

The aching still remains, though, even when I head down the sidewalk and away from the sunrise, leaving it all behind just like my mother did. Through the pain, I keep going, telling myself it's for the best.

If Micha really is the love of my life, I'm doing him a huge favor.

The best thing I can do for him and everyone else, including myself, is leave.

They're much better off without me.

Chapter 13

Micha

After I get out of the shower, I tug a clean shirt over my head then grab my car keys and wallet. I spent last night at Ella's house but barely got any sleep, too riled up and worried to shut my eyes. Before the sun started to come up, I snuck over to my house to clean last night's rainstorm—and memories—off me. But I'm ready to get back to her, worried to leave her for more than a few minutes.

I grab extra clothes to take with me. Last night, I made a promise to myself that I was going to stick by her side until we got through this. She's not going to be alone in that home. She's going to know that she's loved. By me.

After tossing the extra clothes and my cologne into a bag, I race out of the house and across the driveway. When I reach the fence line, I pause. Something feels off. Different. Wrong.

I glance around at Ella's house, my house, the yards, the sleeping neighborhood. Nothing seems out of the ordinary. Perhaps I'm just being paranoid.

As I climb up the tree to get to her window, though, the paranoid feeling only intensifies. When I duck into the room, worry, panic, and fear consumes me.

Her bed is empty.

"No." I run through the house in a panic but can't find her anywhere.

I call her phone. Nothing. Go back to her room, but she's still not there.

The closer I look, the more I realize that she might not be coming back. Some of her stuff is gone. Clothes are scattered everywhere. The duffel bag in her closet isn't there. And her sketchbook is missing

It hits me like a blow to the chest, cutting so deeply, I think my heart actually cracks.

I fight to breathe.

Ella is gone.

Without me.

And she might not be coming back.

About the Author

Jessica Sorensen is a *New York Times* and *USA Today* bestselling author that lives in the snowy mountains of Wyoming. When she's not writing, she spends her time reading and hanging out with her family.

Other books by Jessica Sorensen:

<u>The Coincidence Series:</u>

The Coincidence of Callie and Kayden

The Redemption of Callie and Kayden

The Destiny of Violet and Luke

The Probabilty of Violet and Luke

The Certainty of Violet and Luke

The Resolution of Callie and Kayden

Unbeautiful (Coming Soon)

Seth & Grayson (Coming Soon)

The Secret Series:

The Prelude of Ella and Micha (Coming Soon)

The Secret of Ella and Micha

The Forever of Ella and Micha

The Temptation of Lila and Ethan

The Ever After of Ella and Micha

Lila and Ethan: Forever and Always

Ella and Micha: Infinitely and Always (Coming Soon)

The Shattered Promises Series:

Shattered Promises

Fractured Souls

Unbroken

Broken Visions

Scattered Ashes (Coming Soon)

Breaking Nova Series:

Breaking Nova

Saving Quinton

Delilah: The Making of Red

Nova and Quinton: No Regrets

Tristan: Finding Hope

Wreck Me

Ruin Me (Coming Soon)

The Fallen Star Series (YA):

The Fallen Star

The Underworld

The Vision

The Promise

The Fallen Souls Series (spin off from The Fallen Star):

The Lost Soul

The Evanescence

The Darkness Falls Series:

Darkness Falls

Darkness Breaks

Darkness Fades

The Death Collectors Series (NA and YA):

Ember X and Ember

Cinder X and Cinder

Spark X and Cinder (Coming Soon)

The Sins Series:

Seduction & Temptation

Sins & Secrets

Lies & Betrayal (Coming Soon)

Standalones

The Forgotten Girl

<u>Coming Soon:</u>

Unraveling You

Entranced

Steel & Bones

Connect with me online:

jessicasorensen.com

http://www.facebook.com/pages/Jessica-Sorensen/165335743524509

https://twitter.com/#!/jessFallenStar

Made in the USA
Middletown, DE
18 April 2017